I0598156

# THE DARKEST LIGHT

Dalton Frey

Copyright © 2017 by Dalton Frey. All rights reserved.

No part of this book may be reproduced, stored in or introduced into any retrieval system, distributed, transmitted into any form by any means (including photocopying, recording, electronic methods, mechanical methods, or otherwise), or used in any manner whatsoever without written permission of Dalton Frey. The exception would be in the case of brief quotations embodied in critical articles, reviews, and pages where permission is specifically granted by the author.

ISBN 978-0-9985741-0-3

# Dedication

I dedicate this book to the Wicked, in the hope that you will one day know peace, love, and understanding, despite all odds.

I dedicate this book to the Just, with the wish that you be rewarded now and forever in accordance to the brilliance of your heart.

I dedicate this book to those who sacrifice for this life, those who would give up their happiness for the world's. May you transcend eternity.

# Acknowledgments

A more than special thank-you goes out to Cody Bannon and Tricia Callahan. Without you both, this novel would not have the life it does.

# THE DARKEST LIGHT

# Chapter 1 – Imagerion

Beliefs, feelings, and effort—these are the great drivers of humanity. Although, it must be stated, they are not the only. Another great engine of change is what is known as imagination: the divine force of the mind we all are capable of harnessing. Imagine for yourself! Is it strange that what does not exist can still be conceived? To think of the impossible is to show what is possible—everything. Those who believe otherwise are not yet edified in the ways of the universe. This is the story of the power of thought; it is also a relation of the strength of volition. The choice of words should not confuse you: nothing that will be stated will be perfect.

This dear story (or should it be said, history?) took place on a planet not really different from the one you are currently hurdling through space on. In fact, the humans, the plants, the animals, and even that physical power referred to as chance were no different. For a time, the planet was almost an exact mirror of what you are accustomed to. Many things were thought. Many questions were asked. Not many answers were given. Strangeness was embodied in the living. How odd is it that all that is existence never bestowed upon the living the abilities they so sought? To think of the impossible is to, perhaps, reveal what is inevitable. Imagination, the power of the mind, was separate from those to whom it belonged. This was, at least, until one day . . . The day everything was realized.

It began with no prelude. At once, it seemed, the universe decided to conspire in favor of sentient beings. For some of the population, it was during the day. For others, it occurred during their dreams. And, when those who were dreaming woke up, they had trouble believing that they really were awake. The event was called Imagerion—it was the union of physical forces and incorporeal forces; it bestowed upon the living a power called Soula. With this skill, all could live their lives in the manner they were always supposed to—or so that is what was said. Soula, brought to fruition by the event Imagerion, gave the living the ability to physically manipulate that which is not living (the exception being plants), in addition to other abilities—so it was taught. With Soula, it was discovered that one could overpower and relinquish another life through the force. Conversely, one could defend themselves with it. Mental links could also be made to share memories and feelings with one another in a manner seemingly unreal. One could use their power to visit, literally, their mental concepts. Beings could sense one another with it. Utilizations were endless. But with these capabilities, human spirits were challenged at a dangerous rate.

Think for yourself! What would you do with this? For the world, it allowed society to advance faster than previously possible. Confusion followed when creativity settled in. Countries' boundaries became blurry; separate cultures and beliefs mingled closer than ever before. Through the eyes of the stars, the world began a period of unprecedented transformation. History tells that the world was not made perfect—though, it may forever strive to be. Imagerion was followed by a series of epochs, which helped to make the world seemingly more complicated than before. Many of the olden ways, embraced by inveterate populations of the past, were tossed out as the world became a more convoluted place where new systems were needed. However, despite these new powers, the force known as malice adapted. While the world was presumably better off than before, it was far from consistent and ideal.

It is here that you must now be thrust into the fray that is this relation. Keep in mind, as timeless as this tale is, time has no degenerative effect on what is to be said. Time does matter, however; be sure to know the difference.

For some, this is where the story begins. For others, the story has already ended.

# Chapter 2 – The Awakening

*There is only inevitability*
*And the pain I will prevent.*
*Hallowed is my mission.*
*Righteous is my vision.*
*Anger is my weapon,*
*For it is my very core.*
*I will save us from us*
*And know serenity forever more.*

The Code of the Falling Sun, of Rasck the Reaper, echoed with the direness of eternity in Zarra's mind. She was a Fearnaught, pledged to protect the living from those agents of evil. And yet, she could not shake the feeling—a numinous feeling—from her body as she stood among the chaos. Before her was Rasck, dressed in the glory of power and flawless triumph, wearing his white robes of purity, advancing without haste; one could even say that he stepped with a serene tenderness. To the Reaper's left and right, members of the Falling Sun marched on with him uninhibited due to his demonstrably omnipotent prowess.

Zarra feared for her life and those whom she was with. It was so haunting to see death approaching her at such a steady rate, flashing in her eyes like a grand alarm. The Sun was even shining, and it was midday. All around her was life: the gently swaying branches of the trees, the sweet rippling of water from the fountain in the town square. There was no way this was actually happening. Strange to say, that is usually how dramatic events happen. With now-labored breathing, she felt weak, helpless. Her body was fatigued and methodically being worn down, to the joy of her aggressors. Panic rained, despite the midday Sun, in the form of terrified souls: people were running about with no regard for anything but survival. Before them was the Reaper, and after him there would be nothing.

Zarra, along with the other Fearnaughts, was attempting to protect the people by warding off the onslaught that was to come, inevitably. Defeating Rasck was not possible; their collective thought, a collective conscious promoted by the sincere situation they had been launched into, was to only slow him to give others the infinitesimal chance of escape. Such a task had never been accomplished before, and the unfolding scene promised no different. The hands of time thrust out, and the Fearnaughts were held in dismay as the ground around their feet caved in, and the Reaper was just outside of comfortable speaking distance. Zarra, noticing the trap forming around her feet, leapt away quickly before the dirt encased her ankles, and sprinted off with the inspiration of fear, empowered by a pulsating heart, behind a corner of buildings and out of sight.

With serious adroitness, she blew down a nearby door and hid inside for cover. The building was deserted, unlike the rest of the town of Lanhauster, which was quickly becoming a war zone. At this time, no breath was being taken by her shaken foundation. Now cognizant of this, she tried to breathe in a controlled manner—impossible. Her eyes, previously out of focus, came to and revealed a staircase. Without knowing why—for who knows why they do what they do when faced with mortal peril—she climbed the stairs with an upright and stiff posture. As she made it through the corresponding environs, a window was soon revealed that overlooked the town square—where she had just been. With determined but scared eyes, she peered out and saw the two opposing forces now facing off. Her companions were wriggling with fervent distaste at their legs, encased to the shin in an unmoving concoction of the ground. The onlooker brought a trembling hand to a quivering mouth as the sight of Rasck advancing toward the trapped overcame all senses and thoughts.

The Reaper walked slowly toward his adversaries, the Sun glistening off his immaculate cloak. Basking in his own shining ecstasy, he spent time looking at each of his captives. No one could tell exactly where his gaze fell, for his head was covered by his robe's hood. His face was shrouded in mystery by a white, cloth mask with a red stripe covering where his eyes would be. Around him, the Order of the Falling Sun stood wearing their matching but bloodred cloaks. For anyone who knew who these people were, the sight would have been enough to overflow their mental state with anxiety.

With screams still in the background and people flying off into the distance using any surface they could, Rasck stood and observed what he saw with genuine curiosity. Oh, how obvious it was! Does evil not cherish their triumphs? There was an air of amusement around him, though it was faint. But, at the same time, there was a hint of sadness. He had won—as usual—without any real opposition. Still, he took only a short time before speaking to the ensnared Fearnaughts. "I'm—I'm sorry. . . ." His voice was so cold, winter itself would have shuddered at the sound. And, strangely, there was a salient articulation in his voice indicative of understanding. "I'm sorry. It's just that . . . as I was on my way here . . . to free you all . . . I couldn't help but notice . . ." At this, he lifted a hand and touched his head. No one there in the square could have understood what he was talking about. "Could you please tell me where the person who did this is?" No one dared to move. "I'd like to congratulate them before I finish up here. I'd never been touched since I became this 'Reaper' you refer to me as. To do so . . . is quite a feat. Quite a feat indeed!" The dichotomous nature of the scene would have made a very pretty picture had it not been for the imminent death. Time was frozen, it seemed, and the only one who could dispel time was the brightened man now walking toward the small group of Fearnaughts. Rasck passed each person, placing his right hand with a loving touch on each face. Of course, he had to take his glove off first. For a mental link to be established using Soula, there must be direct contact with the bodies being linked. "Hmm . . . so no one knows. Such a shame! I really was looking forward to meeting that individual. . . ." Strides past the group were made by the interlocutor. He made a motion as if he were taking a deep breath. Who would have known such a villain still needed to do something as hygienic as breathing?

Nodding at everything he was surveying, he continued. "Well then . . . this was fun. . . . I envy each of you. Moving on beyond this abysmal world . . . Oh, how I wish I could join you. . . . One day I will, that is true. Even the Reaper will need his rest. But at least, for now, we can spend some bonding time together.

Behold . . . the pulse!" At this, an enormous pulse was emitted from him and momentarily turned everything a slight tint of red. "Ah . . . there everyone is." He turned and walked back to the initial spot of his initiation at a reasonable pace. At the wave of his hand, a great scythe appeared before him from the sky. It was an instrument of his, appropriately named Mercy. For him, it was an emancipator. For others, it was . . . well, an entity of the abyss, so to speak.

Zarra's heart stopped as he held it up high in the air—she knew what was to come next. But, it wasn't for that reason a fresh new sense of dread snuck up on her. It was the sight of a little girl making her way toward Rasck. Correspondingly, Mercy was lowered, and its wielder made his way to the newly revealed soul. "Why . . . hello there, little one. I felt your presence, but why did you come out? You must be very brave, truly."

The little girl, with her rosy cheeks and curly hair, stood there watching him for a moment. She then asked, in a petite voice, "I know who you are. All of my friends say you're mad. . . . But if that's true, how comes I can feel that you are sad?"

"Perceptive, little one . . . very perceptive. Well, I am a being of truth. . . . I am sad. In fact, I have been for quite some time. And what I do makes me sad, very, very much so. Yet, I have to do it— it's what needs to happen. And for that reason, what I do also makes me happy."

"But why?"

"Why, indeed. . . . Before you are saved, my dear, I have a question for you. I always like to ask at least one person before a cleansing." He moved toward her and knelt down. Behold! The Reaper with a small, innocent child. Save a more terrible sight! He asked her, in a voice barely audible, "Why do you live?" The little girl looked at him, indifferent. Without needing much time to think, she then whispered her answer to the side of his head.

"Ah . . . what a reason. . . . Good. Very good! Thank you, my dear, for sharing." He stood up and raised Mercy to the heavens. A terrible, booming noise filled the air, and Zarra lost consciousness as her mind softly fell into a horribly serene stupor.

# Chapter 3 – The Awakened

Zarra opened her eyes. All that was seen was darkness—nothing. Her body, the extension of her life, ached. Grinding her teeth, she pulled herself up to a sitting position and tried to take her surroundings into account. Quickly each sense was tested. All of them were completely intact, although a little weakened. "Am . . . am I dead?" she wondered. She quickly got to her feet and whirled her head around. No sight of the Reaper or Falling Sun. Rather, there was no sight of anything. She then said aloud, in a panic, to a monstrous echo, "AM I DEAD?" The words bounced around her and engulfed her as her knees crumbled downward.

Suddenly she felt the ground beneath her change its texture. A stream of water was just in the distance—she could hear it. The smell of sweet plants and fresh air filled her nostrils, and her eyes opened to a figure standing under one of the nearby trees. It was the figure of a man, a bit taller than average, clothed in a strange outfit colored dark green and gray. The being had on brown boots, and everything he was wearing was made of a material unknown to her. She got to her feet and saw his face, sporting a small smile, looking back at her. His pale skin, dark eyes, and dark brown hair, and the little birthmark on the side of his left cheekbone were familiar to her. She exhaled. "No . . . I don't believe it. I've seen you before!" Zarra's mind began to race as the confusion from everything that had happened to her was overwhelmed by what was now before her. "I know who you are! You're—"

"I am Deceus Stormeus Maximus," the man said, and nodded.

"You're . . . You're—"

"The Angel and the Orator . . . Those are two other names I am called, yes. And your name is?

"Zarra. My name is Zarra. I'm a Fearnaught."

Zarra still couldn't make sense of her predicament. She by no means was unintelligent; it was a refusal of a dreaded thought. A moment ago she was about to be slaughtered by the Reaper's ability to kill with Soula. A second ago she was in some kind of enchanted space where she couldn't see anything. And now, she was seeing a man about whom she had heard stories all of her life. This being, named Deceus Stormeus Maximus, called the Angel and the Orator, was from many, many years ago. Yet, he now appeared to only be in his early thirties.

With belief, she stated, "I must be dead."

"Fear not, Fearnaught. You are not dead. You are very much, as one would say, 'alive.'" This certainly did not help to clear up the situation; her countenance revealed that. "Before I explain what has happened, would you like something to eat? A drink too, I think, would be in order." Raising his hand, he created a small table complete with two chairs out of the nearby materials. "There is a very nice assortment of natural foods here. For example, the stream is very clean." At this, he pulled water from the stream and placed it into cups, which he had also made on the table. "And, the plants have been most generous." Two plates were crafted simultaneously with wood from a nearby tree. Floating through the air, an assortment of food drifted into the scene and settled in a picturesque way on the table.

Deceus sat down and spoke with great cordiality. "Please, join me."

Birds could be heard chirping happily in the distance. A small woodland creature ran across tree branches in splendor. Zarra, relaxing the confounded expression off her face, obliged to sit down. For her, it was more out of curiosity than anything else. It did take a couple of moments for her to realize that she was truly safe and that no harm could come to her; her background as a Fearnaught, though brief, was always present in one form or another. Only after she sat down and got comfortable did Deceus decide to reach for his cup and take a drink. No doubt, he was contemplating her thoughts at the time. "Now, I can imagine you have many, many questions. In time, I will reveal everything to you. But, for now, we will address one thing at a time. Feel free to interrupt me should you have a question. Yes?"

"I—yes." The Fearnaught took a piece of fruit and examined it for a second before taking a bite. Only now did she realize how hungry she was: her stomach was too preoccupied with elaborate and dire thoughts earlier for it to be aware of itself.

With the two now eating at a leisurely pace, the stream flowing happily, and the sounds of nature emitting a shroud of tranquility around them, Deceus began. "Now, I will be quick in speaking and short on the details. You are correct. I am who you think I am. I was just a few years older than you when Imagerion happened. Yes . . . I lived in a time where we did not have Soula. Needless to say, I became very skilled with it in a very short amount of time. I have no shame in admitting that I was absolutely fascinated by it. I had so many questions: 'Why now? Why at all? What? How?' I studied Soula with the upmost care and consideration possible. There were many, many questions that I had. Despite my expertise, I could not answer all of them. Fast-forwarding, I froze myself with the help of some very erudite, scientific people so that if the world would ever need me, I could come back. The condition was simple: I would only be reawakened by a force powerful enough to sensitize my Soula-generated barrier. No doubt, the abilities of this individual called Rasck were powerful enough to break the barrier. Why it did not break sooner considering all that has happened, I cannot say. Upon my awakening, I was rather weak. You must understand, when one reanimates after such a hibernation it takes time for them to regain their strength. However, I sought out the source that I felt. That is what led me to you."

"Me?" Zarra asked.

"Yes, you. After I accomplished a link with Rasck, I tried to filter through all of the information that flooded my mind. However, it became very apparent that I needed time and that extreme focus was required. I was trying to sort through everything that I exposed myself to as I was making my way through the town when I entered a building next to the square. There, I entered a room and saw you watching . . . what we both saw. I mustered what strength I had when I saw that Rasck was about to slay everyone, and it was enough for me and you to escape. I regret to say I couldn't take anyone else. . . . It was a very dangerous maneuver that only a few people in my time, I think, could have done. It involved us blasting up into the sky at a rate so fast that we were able to get out of Rasck's range of death. You see, he opted to fire out as far and wide as he could. He did not bother, or so I guess, to extend his range far into the heavens."

"You made a link with Rasck?!" Incredulity could be heard in the words. "That's incredible! Do you know what that means? We can learn about him now! Anyone can!" Zarra's mood suddenly lifted immensely. She was no stranger to death, but recent events still took a large toll on her. Despite her ability to fight off the aftershock, she could not keep her excitement at bay at this news; not all of the equanimity in the world could have. She then asked the more important question. "How did you do it? There's no way . . . you couldn't have gotten close enough to touch him to establish a link."

Deceus smiled. To do so is often a hallmark of wise men who are always pleased that the acts they do seem impossible. "Zarra, how much do you know about me?"

"I—I know a good bit. I know most about your actions in New Hope City." She blushed, now realizing that she was face-to-face with a historical figure who was held in high esteem.

"Then, you must know what this is?" He reached down his shirt and pulled out a gold-and-green-tinted object that dully reflected the world around it.

# Chapter 4 – The Mirrored Locket

What Zarra saw was a locket. It appeared to be normal, but she knew better than to base her judgment on appearance alone. "I've seen pictures of it before."

Again, Deceus smiled, pleased at the news. "Tell me everything you know about Rasck."

"Why? You made a link with him. You have to know more than I—"

"Not yet . . . You know what I do not. You know how people see him, whereas I cannot perceive him in the conventional sense. . . . I need to understand how the world sees him, not how I see him. Start from the beginning, please. Take me through his inception to where he is today. It is important that these things are discussed rather than transferred from a link."

The two sat with relative silence between them as the Fearnaught thought. She closed her eyes. "He . . . No one knows his real name. No one knows who he is. They only know him by Rasck, but no one knows if that's his actual name or if it's just what he designated for himself. . . . There is a city on the west coast named Manestay. That's—That's where it all started."

"Manestay, you say?" He then whispered, "The birthplace of the Medical Revolution?"

"The what?"

"Please, continue."

Zarra stopped to think again. "One day the entire city of Manestay was wiped out. Gone because of him and his power. All of its people, I mean. He didn't bother with anything else, just the people." Deceus's eyes narrowed at this. "He's been nicknamed the 'Reaper' because he kills everyone and because he carries a scythe . . . named Mercy." Deceus's head gave a slight nod. "Ever since then, he's been moving from the west coast to the east coast, going north and south along the way . . . killing everyone. Well, not everyone . . . There's some who decided to join him. They're the other ones you saw dressed in red who were with him. They're called the Falling Sun." With this, Deceus gave an imperceptible exhale.

"What do people think about him? What do they say?"

"They say he's unstoppable. People have tried, but it has been decided . . . yes, decided . . . that people are to stay where they are and defend against him if—when, I mean—he comes."

"Why?"

"Well, it's thought that if people defend where they are from, it will give them an advantage. They are protecting what they love— their home. Personally, I can't see it. I think that it's just a way of slowing him down. It takes time for him to move from one location to the next. If we put everyone in one place for him, we'd be boxing ourselves in—cornering ourselves for the fatal swipe of his Scythe."

"And everyone adheres to this rule?"

"No. Some have fled to other places around the globe, some stay where they are . . . but people like me especially do not."

"The Fearnaughts?"

"Yes." Zarra couldn't help but feel proud by this. It was her commitment, her sacrifice. A being of action must be rooted in something, otherwise it may fall for anything. "We are a group of people from all over the globe who wish to see his downfall. . . . We want to take action rather than sit around and hope for the solution to just appear. Headquartering in Lowhi, we established a force of like-minded people who act on their own accord." She pointed to her outfit. "This is what each of us wears to signify who we are." Zarra wore a black uniform with some green accents. With it, a green belt, and the Tree of Live clearly shown on her left sleeve just below her shoulder—the symbolic tree of Lowhi. The green of the belt and the tree matched her eyes, and her dirty blond hair contrasted nicely with the overall presentation. "As of late, we have been sending out troops in waves to locations we think he will hit next." She suddenly shifted her eyes downward, and her voice softened. "It was my turn. . . . That's why I was at Lanhauster."

A swift breeze cut through, shaking the leaves and branches in a mystic way. Silence ensued in the form of mutual understanding.

Not only between the two people but between all the natural life there; it was an act of admiration.

Deceus broke the silence—it was what was needed for time to progress during such spells. "Rasck is feared."

"He's not just feared. He's . . . He's beyond that. Fear is just an instrument of his. His image is an infection: it makes him more powerful. We've seen what he can do. Entire populations have crumbled in a manner of seconds before him. He just goes and uses his Soula to sense and lock on to every person within the radius, and just like that everyone is gone. Of course we're afraid of him. He can sense everything and block everything. We can't kill him by other means either. It'd be too easy for him to redirect something like a bomb; it could only work in his favor. Biological weapons also don't work. It's like he knows everything about them. Our only chance is beating him with Soula."

"Perhaps. . . . Perhaps not. Time will tell, as it usually does. We do, in the meantime, still have to act." Deceus took off the Locket, which was hanging on his neck, and put it on the table. "A Soullex is an object unique to whom it belongs: it is an article of meaning to them. With it, a person can become stronger in the ways of Soula if the Soullex in question has meaning to them with their current task. No doubt, Mercy is Rasck's Soullex—the Scythe. It has meaning to him—a meaning of death, I presume—and because of that, it helps him to kill. Is that term still in fashion? Soullex, I mean."

"Yes. We still use it." Zarra knew all too well what a Soullex was. Many people had at least one. The term, after all, was first coined by the man sitting before her.

"Well then, this is a Soullex. It, however, has a very unique ability and one that, to my knowledge, has not been replicated. As you know, when a mental link is formed between two people using Soula, both parties surrender their internal worlds to the other. In other words, one cannot obtain information from the other without surrendering themselves as well. This"—he pointed to the Locket—"gives the wielder the ability to form a mental link with another person without physical contact and without surrendering information. All one has to do is open it and use the mirror to see the reflection of the desired person. Also, if one were to look into the mirror and see their own reflection, it can show them their true self—who they really are."

Zarra's eyes widened. "How is that possible? I've never heard of such a thing. But that's how you did it? That's how you formed a link with Rasck?"

"That is a tale for another time—a time in which my past days at New Hope will be revealed to you. And yes, it is. I've also found out that a person can use it to store and share selected memories, mental constructs, and so forth with another without forming the link."

Zarra, in her appreciation of the object, got eager. What laid before her had all of the information she would ever need to defeat Rasck. "Let me see it," she said. "I want to know who he is. I want to know how to beat him."

Deceus could hear the acrimony. "Your vindictiveness is understandable, but I fear that it strays from the true path, Fearnaught. On the table lies the internal world of a very twisted man, whose memories, feelings, and thoughts will be too much for anyone who is not inoculated to such things to bear. I do not doubt your abilities; I simply trust Rasck's strength. If you will, you can try it. But you must be prepared to deal with the repercussions."

A feeling of presumptuousness entered the Fearnaught. The thought of being able to understand the most hated man in the world was too good to simply give up! Only a fool would think otherwise. She reached for the Locket, felt the metal on her skin, brought it up, and began the link.

Zarra immediately shut down. Her journey in Rasck's mind lasted for only an ephemeral amount of time. A searing agony began in her chest—her heart—and shot through the rest of her body almost instantaneously. It was no more comfortable than falling through a poisonous atmosphere lit on fire. A premature release was forced.

And she began to spiral back to the pleasant scene where Deceus was waiting for her. She was falling and falling and falling with gravity pulling her down ever so roughly. A stark contrast existed between the world she was in and the world she just tried to see. The dichotomy was too much to handle when she came to her senses; she felt depressed . . . and angry. "What . . . What was that?" she whispered.

Deceus cast an intent look at her. "Rasck is not just a brute; he's intelligent. He feared that someone would try to understand him, so he put a defense mechanism upon himself. I've known some people to do this before but not like what you just experienced. What did you see? Feel?"

"I . . . I saw nothing. No matter how hard I tried, there was just . . . nothing." An involuntary shudder coursed through the Fearnaught. "I just felt—"

"Indescribable?"

"Indescribable. Have you tried?"

"As soon as I could. Some was learned, but it will take time to get through everything. His most precious memories and ones he deemed most important at the time of the link will be the most heavily guarded." Deceus stood up and walked over to the stream. While he was gazing at his own reflection, the still seated took the time to take another drink. The Sun was setting in the distance, and night was soon to come. "Zarra, I need you to understand something."

Zarra didn't answer; she knew that she didn't need to.

"You are here today because of the actions you have taken. It was not destiny that you would appear before me; it was a string of decisions you made. Rather than accepting inaction, you took action. Instead of fleeing the Reaper, you faced death. I have every intention of stopping the man by exploring his past and revealing who exactly is behind the red visor." There was a hint of reflection in his eyes. "If you wish to destroy something, you should understand it first. . . ."

"Are you asking me to join you?"

The Angel turned from the water and faced her. "I could never *just* ask someone to do what lies ahead. You will see some of the most terrible acts in human history, things that far surpass our greatest fears. I am, however, giving you the opportunity to join me—and teach you. Your actions led you here, Zarra. And I don't think that you would ever cease to act until the malice known as Rasck is abolished. If you decide to join me, a clear distinction must be made—a great realization. You will do what you will do because it is what you *choose* to do, not what you are *destined* to do."

"Is there that much of a difference?"

"The greatest."

30

Zarra paused to let his words sink in. There is something eerily ominous in such moments of aberration. And yet, in all things, there can be found a spark of serendipity. She proclaimed, "I will. I will join you, and I will do what it takes to help."

Again, her interlocutor gave a small smile, which lasted for only a second. The Sun continued to dip in the sky as nighttime approached. "I believe you. Right now, we are west of Lanhauster. Rasck is advancing to the east, and since he wages genocide on everything before him, he will not bother to turn to what is behind him. So long as we stay to this side and advance in conjunction with the Falling Sun and not cross their path, we should be reasonably safe. Of course, the power of one's Soula diminishes over distance. Although, his range is most formidable."

"What will we do?"

"Tomorrow, Fearnaught, we will learn."

# Chapter 5 – The Journey

The next day, Deceus and Zarra set off on foot toward the east. Instead of traveling by making and manipulating objects using Soula, Deceus insisted that they traverse the land. This was to Zarra's distaste. She knew that the Reaper was traveling over the lands using his Stone Throne—a literal throne he made from stone, which he sat on while traveling—and couldn't see why they should tire themselves out by walking. However, it was said that an explanation would be given at the end of the day. So, looking forward to discovering why, she walked with him through the lands, sticking to natural paths and staying away from where civilization could be found.

The two talked about how far Rasck had come through the continent. There were five major cities: Manestay, Allelse, Venestag, Sumeq, and Lowhi. The first two had succumbed to his wrath. With the recent downfall of Lanhauster, a smaller city in a centralized location, he was already halfway across the continent. After that conversation, however, Deceus and Zarra refrained from talking. Deceus needed to focus on breaking through Rasck's memories. Conversing would not have helped with that arduous task. So, the day progressed with silence between the two and the music of the winds to fill the void. Through fields and hills alike, they created their own path. It was spring: a plethora of natural life was blooming as if their planet were waking from a deep sleep. Despite her comforting natural surroundings, Zarra couldn't help but feel annoyed, impatient. Like most, she was a failing to appreciate the long-term rewards afforded by her short-term costs. Walking with a clenched, grinding jaw and hardened hands, she felt the day wear on her slowly, like chains periodically being added to her shoulders. *He must know how vexed I am*, she thought. *I can feel it. What lesson is this? I'm learning nothing! Nothing at all.*

***

At last, with the Sun starting to descend behind them, Deceus spoke. "We will rest here tonight." Without making any physical movement, he crafted two small huts out of the natural supplies around him for the two to use as shelter. Between the huts, two chairs were made, and they sat down. Soula, it should be said, can be used solely by using one's mental faculties. However, combining that with physical movements could make it more powerful.

*Finally*, Zarra thought as she plopped down with a sigh. Her legs ached, not used to such a trek. Her companion, however, sat without a sound, lost in mental musing. His countenance had a shade of concentration as he stared off into the distance. Only the sounds of nature decorated the airwaves with light dimming.

At length, Deceus broke the silence as he returned to their world. "I apologize that I cannot be more cordial. Rasck's mind is our priority, and that is where my efforts must lie."

"Why did we have to walk?" There was a hint of annoyance in the Fearnaught's voice. "Come to think of it, why don't we just fly over him and the Falling Sun? They won't chase us if we go in the direction they plan on going anyway. We should have done that. . . . I feel so stupid!" She buried her hands in her face. "We are wasting so much time!"

Deceus gave her a mild glance, a signal that she took to reserve herself. "You're a woman of action, Zarra. I cannot help but sympathize with you. While we are making our way through fields and forests, your friends are out trying to make a difference."

"And now we are just sitting here." Evidently, the day's frustration was now leaking.

"That's right, now we are just sitting here. But now I have the opportunity to tell you why we are doing what we are doing." His answer was calm and lacked indignation. At these words and the way they were spoken, Zarra became self-aware. She didn't show her regret for lashing out, but it was known that it was in there, somewhere. "Patience is a very underrated strength. There are times for immediate action, and there are times when action would be detrimental. You are right to challenge me, but do not do so out of emotional strife."

"I'm sorry." She paused. "But why are we walking?"

"Are you familiar with how Soula is powered?"

"Of course. We are taught from a young age! Soula is activated by our mind and can be used with our thoughts. And, if we move our bodies in conjunction with our thoughts, it can become more powerful. The three factors that affect the strength of Soula are beliefs, feelings, and effort. The stronger one believes in something, the stronger they become. The more powerful the emotions one possesses, the more power they gain. And, the more effort one gives with Soula, the better they are with it. Inconsistencies between the trio, though, can interfere with your abilities. Soullexes have their parts too."

Deceus nodded. "Correct. All three must be used to the maximum for our mission—anything less will result in certain failure. Emotions will come from our experiences in Rasck's past and mental constructs I plan on sharing with you; they'll also come from within. Beliefs will form based on how we decide to think. Effort, however—"

"—will come from how hard we push ourselves . . . and practice." Zarra suddenly understood. The journey they were on, as tedious as it was, would make them more powerful over time. "If you were to pit two people against each other who had the same beliefs and emotions, but one traveled to the battle with Soula and the other through physical exertion . . . assuming everything was equal . . . the latter would win."

"Undoubtedly. It will likely take Rasck about a month and a half to destroy everything on this continent before he moves on to the next. Since we will be moving more slowly, we can move in a straight line while he and the Falling Sun zip north and south just ahead of us."

"Before he moves on to the next continent?" Zarra had been so concerned about what would happen if he should reach Lowhi, she had not given much consideration to what would happen if the Scythe moved on.

Deceus took a deep breath before saying, "Yes." The nearby leaves swayed, and all animals alike stopped as if they heard and understood what was said—such is the effect of a symphony that suddenly freezes. Deceus took out his Locket and held it resolutely in his hand. "I promised you that we would learn. Now, we begin." Holding out the Locket to the Fearnaught, he exclaimed, "Hold on to it with me, and you shall see." Zarra grasped the Locket and closed her eyes as the feeling of ascension flowed in her veins.

***

The Angel and the Fearnaught were transported into a mental construct of the former's. The latter opened her eyes to a misty room with a calming light-blue-tiled floor and black ceiling that appeared to be the night sky. There wasn't a cloud in the distance, and the stars shone brightly like candles contrasted against the dark above. It was pleasantly warm, comfortable. A little way away, she saw the Orator moving across the room.

"Our minds are beautiful, aren't they?" he whispered. Although to her, it sounded like he was right next to her. "Look up! See the night sky! Marvel at the mystery that is our universe, and bask in the serenity that is space and time. And then, behold!" The entire room was now surrounded by mirrors.

"Where are we?" Zarra asked with a rush of alacrity. She had seen and been in mental constructs before, but something felt special about this one. There was a sense of repose and criticalness at the same time, a mixture of feelings otherwise mutually exclusive. Infirmity was not possible here, only possibility. "I—I feel torn. Like my zeal is at its zenith, but so is my anxiety."

"This is a creation of mine. Let us call it 'The Mirror of Men.' It is a representation, a most appropriate artistic collection of history. It is this that Rasck has sought to understand throughout his life—that is clear."

"These mirrors"—the objects gleamed like foggy pearls— "what do they do?"

"Discover for yourself. Gaze at them, and you shall see. Think about them then, and you can understand."

Zarra walked up to a mirror and placed a hand on its cool surface. Instantaneously, a phantasmagoria flashed upon the mirror and scattered to all of the others, which were in a circle around them. She heard a polyphonic array fill the room, tenaciously and without constraint. As she stepped back and turned around, it began to flood her senses: her mind was swimming with information and wonder. "What is this?"

"A timeline . . . A timeline of history and everything that has happened in human existence." He too began to circle around her. "Tell me, what do you see?"

"I see . . . I see discoveries being made. . . . I see people fighting. . . . I hear people laughing and crying. . . . I hear music. . . . I see cultures . . . the fruition of missions . . ."

"What about patterns?"

Zarra's heart rate slowed amid the grandeur of the misty, mirrored room. Her focus sharpened—pieces and formations previously hidden appeared. "There's a pattern, cyclical . . . a cyclical pattern." She took another moment to allow processing. "It's like a pendulum . . . bouncing all around without any true, fixed route. But it moves toward the one side and then back toward the other. . . . A continuum? Maybe a wave?"

The Orator responded, "There are many ways this can be represented. That is the complexity of our reality. By nature, it's truly formless—fluid. But even then, there is no gravity providing it direction. What gives it direction are the same things that guide us— beliefs, feelings, and effort. These are the pillars of our history, and these pillars are built by us. You are right. What you see before you is joy and despair, hope and fear, love and hate, falsehood and truth. Rasck hates our history—it's anathema to him. He looks at this and sees nothing. To the Reaper, there is no reason, only inevitability. There is no meaning, only a cycle that ends in pain. His Code is clear on this."

Zarra thought back to Lanhauster: the echo of death's mantra was still in her mind.

"The world is what we see it to be. Rasck views it as an abomination, immoral." The Orator glanced up at the mirrors, still showing their stories. "He has learned all that he could about the world."

"But why?"

"To find something that would redeem the world he sought to judge."

"But he is acting against everything."

"Which leads me to believe he found nothing."

"So that's it, then?"

"Hardly."

"So what if our history isn't the greatest? What matters is now. He can't justify killing everyone based on the past."

"No. He is justifying killing everyone based on the future."

"I still don't—" Zarra turned to Deceus but did not see him; she was alone in the mirrored room with the mist thickening around her. In a cool breeze, it began to clear, and before her stood only one mirror—it was her size. Only a reflection was shown, green eyes staring back at themselves. She appraised the situation with natural curiosity before the answer formed within her. "He sees the world. . . . He has looked at its history. . . . He sees the patterns . . . but he doesn't see it with meaning. To the corruption within, there is one inexorable fact: pain. There is anger, but it is guided, focused."

The room boomed, "Anger is the emotion of change. There are others but none like it. It is for that reason that many revolutionary epochs are brought forth from the soil with the seeds of rage. That inner rage is watered with tears, heated by hot rays of constant passion from a source seemingly out of reach. One day, it blooms into an explosion of colors, manifested usually in the color red. It lashes out with the feelings of those tears, empowered by the heat of forces various."

"He said he was sad!"

"Nothing could be truer."

"Then what does he want, really?"

"To eliminate negative emotions, dear Fearnaught. The 'cleansing' of what is deemed morose: life. The Reaper seeks to destroy first what can destroy him—other humans. Then, he will eradicate natural life found in our great plains, towering mountains, and deepest oceans, thereby ensuring no life could ever exist here again. Dear Fearnaught, he has seen history. He wishes to end it." And at those final words, the mirror before Zarra shattered.

\*\*\*

The sight of their camp for the night once again came into Zarra's view. Deceus was examining his Locket in thought; such moments of seclusion can result in thoughts most edifying. "Evil oftentimes thinks itself to be good. But, it is more so inconsistent with self-evident laws. Men and women alike have been plagued by a false perception of good throughout all of history—not everyone, let me be clear. To those infected with vice, what they do is usually what they consider justified; it is sometimes moral to them or even thought of as a duty. Rasck and the Falling Sun both are burdened by their 'calling.' The cycle, which 'The Mirror of Men' showed, is the future Rasck wishes to prevent. It, to him, is a history filled with fluctuating pain but always ending in pain. But you must see: it is more than physical pain; it's psychological pain, spiritual pain, a brightly lit specter that haunts us even in the middle of day. However, the hunter fails to regress back to where it all begins. He may succeed in ridding people of their bodies, but there is much more to our identities than this crude matter." He clenched his hand.

"So if he couldn't feel pain, would that solve the problem?" The Fearnaught smiled. "I mean, I can make sure he feels nothing again if he'd like."

Her words prompted a stern look. "Vengeance is *not* the answer." Deceus's eyes had a glint of reflection in them. "And no, it is much more complicated than that."

"What? This isn't about vengeance? My . . . you even said that he plans on exterminating all life! He's killed so many people already! And if what you say is true, even the trees right here won't last if he succeeds! This is about ending him outright, saving the world in the process!"

The Angel shook his head but remained silent. With this silence, the perplexed was drawn into more conversation.

"You think I'm wrong?"

A solemn countenance answered with the passion of experience. "You know what happened at New Hope City. You've heard of it. Vengeance is bred from anger, and anger is—"

"—the emotion of change. Right, I remember, but—" she said, and then suddenly stopped. Flashes of a coliseum entered her mind. Pings of metal against metal rang true in her head, like a sharp bell. Once again, she took the time to remember his past.

Deceus, noting this, picked up. "There are two ways anger can lead to change. The first form is the most common form—the negative variation. It promotes violence, and cunning, and deceit. Since ancient times, it has been viewed as the impetus of malice and ignoble behavior. However, there is a second path that can be taken with anger—the good path. Anger is energy manifested within us. The secret to it, then, is harnessing the energy for good, for motivation to do right. Too many times the seduction of the former route takes hold in our bones. Vengeance is *not* the answer, because it is the *wrong* way to view the situation before us. Again, the world is how you view it. Likewise, so are our actions. Out of revenge, do this not. Let me be clear, our goal is to stop Rasck, not end him where he stands."

"But not following through could be cessation of life!"

"Following through would be the inception of meaningless life. Too often, we dream of changing the world. Rather, we must first change ourselves. You cannot ever think about saving the planet; that is the wrong thought. We can save the world, but if the world is ninety-nine percent gone, how much have we let go?

Instead, be concerned about saving *the next*, whatever that next is. Then, and only then, may you keep the whole that we are. I will not lie to you. It is almost a certainty that many more will be separated from their physical form before we are done. Our only chance is to save the next."

"And what is the next?"

"The last."

The Fearnaught shook her head. To her, what the Orator spoke didn't make sense. "I don't understand."

"You will. But for now, rest. We go again tomorrow."

With that, the two went to bed as the shroud of night sleepily rolled over above.

# Chapter 6 – A Time When

Over the next couple of days, Zarra became more appreciative of their journey. She wished she could have communicated with the world what she was learning, but to do so would be to expose the secret that she and Deceus had insight into Rasck's past. If it were to ever cross the Reaper that the person who broke into his mind was still alive, it would spell disaster for them; their only advantage would become known, and they, no doubt, would become hunted.

For many people, it is easy to not act. All of the little facets and vicissitudes of life make deeds too energy consuming; to universal detriment, it is an opportunity cost that many are not willing to pay. It was painful for the Fearnaught, so accustomed to immediacy, to wait. Agents of evil were crossing her lands, laying fire and ruin to the pillars of society. What person of well-intentioned heart could bear to know this and be willing to show constraint? But, the controlled manner and expertise of her mentor gave her strength. Upon their first couple of interactions, Zarra challenged Deceus; the challenger now saw that her complaints, though welcomed by the defendant, were unfounded. Many leaders would have lashed back. Yet he, in his equanimity, let her see that he was worthy. There was no forced decision, for it was a conclusion reached by her own volition—an appraisal that led her to only venerate instead of abnegate.

Now in her eyes was a man who was, to her, much more than she deserved to learn from. On their walks, though he still remained laconic to sift through Rasck's mind, he periodically taught her, especially during breaks that they took to eat. His skill with Soula was impeccable, yet ever so gentle. He sought to understand before he judged. His methods were seemingly unfounded, yet a simple conversation with him would reveal logic previously inconceivable to those not as holistic. Zarra felt ashamed at the world for turning away from the man's teachings. He had given the world answers that would have led to an era of prosperity, yet those answers were cast off for degradation. The cycle of history decided to intervene once again to break a positive trend. For these reasons, among many others, she learned to appreciate him fully and now was wholly committed to traversing forward to that descending star. This wasn't about saving, that cliché article of almost every legend. No, this was about something far greater.

***

Dusk came, which they usually walked through, but today Deceus stopped early. As before, their lodgings were made from their surroundings, determined to only be in place for the night and be reinstated to their original places in the morning. With the Sun setting slowly, the field they were now in gleamed with golden and orange rays. Like the rolling tides of the ocean, the gales of nature breezed through, making the land look as if it were really water. The Angel was quiet, rocking back in forth in his chair. Out of respect, his companion did not stir conversation, patiently waiting.

"Why did you join the Fearnaughts?"

The sudden question reeled the questioned out of the picturesque surroundings. Time was taken to think of the true answer, not one which barely penetrates far into the unconscious. She let out a sigh as she continued to ponder why the question came now. "I'm afraid. I was, well . . . am . . . fearful."

"Of?"

"Regret."

"Why?"

"Because of my lineage. My parents aren't exactly viewed favorably. Their past became my story when I was little and is something I've spent my life trying to overcome. They didn't act in a time of need, and people suffered because of it. That stigma carried over to my existence as I became the one who belongs to 'them.' And I . . . I just didn't . . . don't want to make the same mistake. I believe that I can make a difference, and so I hold myself responsible to that. My parents have been trying to erase the past, and so am I. This is my way of doing it."

"And with no Soullex on hand, at that."

Zarra started to become used to these correct but never-before-addressed facts; this one amazed her. It was just assumed that everyone had at least one Soullex. Yet, he knew she had none on her. In truth, to her knowledge, she didn't really have one.

Deceus stated, "They don't have to become something physical, per se." He smiled. "You know, one of the issues I focused on was the equality of our youth."

"What do you mean?"

"The structure of our society created inequality—in the *sense*—from birth. Some would be born to families of great power and wealth, while others were not. Opportunity was bought from children based on decisions made before them, something which I disagree with. The equality being talked about here—equal opportunity—aimed to ensure people could only be made inequitable—again, in the *sense*—based on themselves. It appears that you, like those, were judged and made unequal based on decisions you had no bearing in—something I call unjust."

"Why did you do it?"

Deceus looked at her to convey that he desired clarification.

"I'm starting to remember everything that I learned about you. What you just said . . . it's all coming back. You fought for equality from the beginning of one's birth, the freedom of choice, the restructuring of justice systems to give criminals value in society.

You pushed forth the importance of nature, questioned monetary systems in the name of economic revolution . . . even created a language that would be used universally. I learned all that you did. But why did you do it?"

"Why, indeed. . . ." The Angel closed his eyes. "I wish that my ideas were taught more than my actions. It was very commonplace for people of physical accomplishments to be celebrated in a greater degree than those of mental faculties back then."

"It still kinda is. . . ."

"Is it?" He showed a small sense of mirth before straightening up in his chair. "To answer your question, I did what I did because I believe in potential. To me, I find it consistent with the laws of the universe. That's why I wrote 'The Axiom of Potentiality.' It was quite polemical, but it served its purpose: progress." Again, the orange-gold ocean gently rippled around them, the plants noising their connections with one another. Deceus asked, "What do you think about not owning a Soullex?"

Zarra shrugged and looked down in obvious indifference. "Can't say. Nothing meaningful really has stuck out to me."

"What about memories?"

"Memories? Ah . . ." She bit her lip in concentration. Suddenly her face lit up, and she looked up, bright teeth gleaming.

"Oh, I definitely have a good one. When I was little, I was trying out a bunch of different hobbies—sports and dancing, really—but there came a time when I was to give a performance, for dancing. And . . . I got up on the stage, right. And I just froze." Deceus had not looked away once during this recital. "I just remember seeing everyone's faces and completely and totally forgetting what it was that I was supposed to do. But then, out of nowhere, I see my father come up onto the stage with me. He assumed the pose"—at this Zarra struck a pose—"and I suddenly remembered everything that I had to do. Turns out, he saw me practicing so much that he memorized my routine. We performed the whole thing together. The audience was just awash in amazement—it was such a happy moment. . . . I eventually gave up dancing for sports, but that moment has always stuck with me and forever will. . . . I can still hear the music playing."

Deceus's eyes focused a bit as he slowly nodded in approval. "Sounds lovely. I suspect that tomorrow I will have something to show you."

Zarra swallowed. "The first bit of Rasck's mind?"

"The first we will see together, yes."

# Chapter 7 – Our Bodies

The next day, around the same time that they stopped the day prior, the two travelers set up camp. The Fearnaught couldn't wait to see what would be shown to her; she had daydreamed about it to pass the time as they ventured. And still, the fear within her was there, carefully boiling under her control. She thought about why she joined the Fearnaughts and what brought her to do so. To many, the motivation brought from fear is our most primal impetus and is therefore reasoned to be the most powerful. Something within her knew this to be wrong, but she couldn't discern what else it could possibly be. The fear of death, the fear of self-image, fear of loss, change, were overtly salient throughout the world. The Fearnaughts chose to reject this philosophy, but no alternative to fear was given as the lever of greatest motivation. Zarra couldn't help but feel fearful and tried in vain to overcome it. Bravery could withstand the task, but bravery increases proportionally to fear. Here, an answer could not be found. She thought of the Fearnaught's code:

"I will not bow

Nor will I break.

All that we are,

I seek to protect and save.

May my bravery guide me

To save the lives I sought.

Come, what may, for I am a Fearnaught."

Over and over, it was recited. Comfort could be found in the words. But it was an island that could not provide or create more than what it already had.

Despite her musings, with lodgings now set up, she sat in meditation to clear her mind. Like the days before, it was a silent day between the two, which promoted calmness. Only today, it had become very overcast and the world appeared rather gray. The darkened world of her inner eyelids shielded an external world that would have otherwise broken concentration. Nothing was heard but a beating heart and slow, controlled breaths, the cool air passing over the tip of her nose.

Suddenly she could feel Deceus's Soula incorporeally beckoning. Her eyes shot open, and the woods around her once again brought in a feeling of closeness. It was true: fear held close to the Fearnaught. Still, the courage within was indomitable, for it was not a matter of infirmity but composure. She got off the tree stump upon which she was sitting and walked back a little to where the Angel was.

He spoke quietly, looking tired but determined. In a tunnel of stress, willpower is the guide out. "I'm learning much, but it is still not nearly enough. What I have is my first major breakthrough."

Zarra went and sat down next to him; a table between the two supported the Locket. "I can't imagine what it's like . . . going through his mind. You must be exhausted. It has to be a waterfall of negativity."

"Only a little."

Zarra appreciated the modicum of humor. "I'm ready."

"Oh, I never would have doubted it." He gave a sly smirk. "What we will see . . . It's far from pleasant, but it gives valuable insight to the first ring."

A quizzical countenance responded. "The first ring?"

"Just the words I chose to use. There are many levels to his defense, but it appears as though the Rasck we know hasn't been like this for long."

"He wasn't always like . . . this?"

"Based on what I have seen, no . . . which leads me to believe that some horrible epoch fell upon the Reaper. Strangely, I sense a lot of positivity . . . and then there's a drop-off point. It's still unclear and needs more time. But, for now, we will witness his destruction of Manestay."

A slight shudder forced itself through Zarra's body; she could feel her hairs starting to stand and the corresponding small bumps on her arms. She half whispered something to herself before relieving the tension in her shoulders.

The Angel placed his hand on the Locket, which was still on the table between them. The environs' grayness made the Locket look a little bit brighter than usual by contrast. "When you're ready," the Angel said.

Zarra hesitated only for a moment before reaching out.

*** 

The five major cities in the land each had their own historic significance. For Manestay, this history was being the center of a Medical Revolution, which brought forth knowledge and technology that would go on to save many lives. To the innocent mother whose child fell ill, her beacon of hope shone to her from its red roofs and tan buildings. Charming architecture could be found here, from times of old with its brick walkways. It was not a poor city nor was it a rich city—it was a happy city. Here, the sky was infused with yellow from the Sun and oceanic blues from the sea. Hardly did rain visit; and, when it did, flowers would be left in its wake. It was never too hot or too cold, but just right most of the year.

The Orator and the Fearnaught found themselves standing in what appeared to be a busy intersection, especially for visitors. It was a large, square clearing in the city that was surrounded by some of the fabled buildings in which discoveries regarding the human body were made. Only a few clouds populated the sky, and the water from an enormous nearby fountain with statues depicting characters of old gleamed from time to time in the fluctuating rays of the Sun.

"Extreme epochs are sometimes preluded by the normality of life. Do you notice anything extraordinary?" the Orator asked.

Zarra looked at the people—of course she could do so freely. Both she and Deceus were visiting this memory in a manner comparable to itinerant ghosts—no one could see them nor feel them, as what was being seen had already passed. There were so many faces moving in a typical mechanical manner, but none looked bothered. Like the movement of the stars, it was a predictable scene that only looked slightly different because of the angle from which it was now being scrutinized. She turned her attention to her entire surroundings—the sky, sounds, buildings—and saw nothing out of normal character. "I don't see anything significant."

"The same observation I have made. And, to the best of your knowledge, was this date historic in any way prior to its destruction?"

"No. That was considered when it happened . . . if it was a result of something before."

The Orator now walked to the middle of the square; the Fearnaught followed. Together, they both were silent and observant. However, Zarra noticed that Deceus's gaze was unwavering. Following his line of sight, she saw him: Rasck the Reaper. He was just sitting on the edge of the fountain, the water behind him gleaming on and off in accordance to the moving shadows of the clouds. The figure was hunched over with forward shoulders, clothed no differently from how the world knew him.

With wide eyes, Zarra asked, "What's he doing?" Even in the mental construct, she whispered in unconscious fear of being heard.

The Orator simply responded, "Thinking. . . . He has been here for quite a while; we came at a time conscious of itself."

Zarra was going to reply, but she saw the daunting figure stand up. She held her breath in vain, as no more action was taken for several moments. That was until, at least, the sky momentarily tinted red. Everyone in the square stopped and looked around, seeking the source. All at once, the blast occurred, and almost everyone collapsed. In the blink of an eye, almost all of the city was gone. Such was the power of the Reaper—a power that shows that it takes years to build but only moments to destroy.

Whirling around, the Fearnaught fought back tears as the impact of being surrounded by motionless bodies rocked her sea of emotions, touching even the deepest internal abyss. In the distance, she could see a man, encased in stone, being held in the air well above head level floating toward Rasck. In bewilderment, the man looked at the white-clad figure and stared into the red band as he neared. Motions were made to escape, but he could not break the spell that had cast the stone together around him.

Looking at her mentor, Zarra mirrored his equanimity and stood firmly as the two watched on. In times of evil, it is important to be defiant to evil, even if that means holding back tears and choosing to stare it in the face.

Mercy, the Scythe, now also floated into view and situated itself in the hand of the main statue of the fountain. The display was disheartening, between the bodies littering the ground and the prisoner floating before a mighty hand. With this, Rasck now spoke as he paced back and forth, gesticulating as if he was deciphering to himself; his helpless and awestruck captive had no choice but to listen to the terrible words.

"Have . . . have you ever considered our bodies? I mean . . . have you ever woken up one day facing your hand and wondered? Opening it slowly . . . and closing it slowly . . . It just seems so . . . so *basic*. It's just such an archaic thing—the body." He jumped into the fountain, splashing as he ran up to the statues. His pace of speech fluctuated and so did his volume. "You see? Look at this!" He ran his shaking hands over them. "Feel it. . . . The primeval matter which constitutes us . . . It's designed to pass away! Uh! Think about it— how fragile we really are!" One of the statues crumbled. "It seems sadistic, like we were meant to be toyed with. Yet we see ourselves as being *so great*. Look here, look at their postures! Chiseled is the detail of the arms and legs and hair. . . . It's a false representation if I ever saw one. And this is not something unique to this time period, no! This has been going on for a long, long time—our boastful attitude toward our bodies. And consider how each of us are made! How . . . mechanical . . . singular . . . ruthless. Yes, ruthless . . . Yes. And what are we? Breathers? Movers? Eaters? Oh, eaters indeed. We sink our teeth into the muscles of other beings, rip the roots out and marinate the soil according to our tastes. What pride could be gathered from that? Our existence depends on the death of others, how horrid . . . how manipulative, grotesque! But hold, look and observe the others whom we share this poisonous atmosphere with. See the other animals? Let them flood your mind—the teeth, skin, hair, and claws . . . everything. Let the flashes of their violence in. . . . See the blood, the gore. Can you now know? Nature is unjust. And we—humans—are no different as we, in all of our misinterpreted grandeur, are part of it still . . . and in more ways than we know! And yet, despite being part of it, we destroy it. Mow down the trees, the grasses! Burn it all to desert and soak up the fluid of life until the moon can no longer stir it!" The Reaper went slowly and sat down at his original spot, shaking his head. With this, the turbulent mood of the situation slowed down. Here, time sped up or slowed down in accordance to that twisted volition. "This world . . .

this life has no mercy. The fibers that weave our existence, our bodies, are threaded without care. We come into this world mechanically. . . . We live throughout this world unjustly. We must kill so we can live, and others must die so that others may live. Here, we strike ourselves down in the form of what extends us: the environment. And what control is there? Even the smallest factors can affect us. . . . Consider our decisions . . . and everything that they are based on. Our implicit, automatic responses plague us from birth and wear us down until the day we return to the memory-less black. . . . Extraneous patterns in the sand and sky disrupt the electricity. . . ." The hooded head now bowed down as the imprisoned man lowered to ground level while a few moments passed. The sight was thus: a helpless man encased by nature facing the Reaper. Surrounding them was death, in the broad daylight of the afternoon Sun, and the normality of life which was, in fact, intentionally serving severity. At last, Rasck spoke. "I have the taste of blood in my mouth." Air filled his lungs with a slow draw, exhibited by a steadily rising chest. While his lungs were filling, he slowly stood at a speed commensurate with the amount of air being brought within. Dramatically, he looked up to the captive through eyes hidden by a white mask with a red stripe. A soft, sleepy voice followed. "Why do you live?"

Writing internally, the man looked incapable of conceiving an answer. Who could have known what was being thought? And who could have known what answer should have been given, if any? As such, nothing was said, and the man simply stared into space.

The Reaper nodded, as if this was an answer. "I see. . . . No one seems to know, it seems. . . ." Those were the last words the stone-clad man heard before Mercy slashed through the sky.

A swift, gray gust of dust swept up and swirled around Zarra and her mentor as they transported away.

\*\*\*

The Fearnaught opened her eyes to a blackened sky. If there was a Sun, it was not here. She looked at the buildings; they looked charred and from a time period she did not recognize. Clearly, this was way before her time. Only the flames spread throughout the dusty, decrepit street gave any light, even though the flames were faint and sickly. "Where—" she began, but stopped to notice her boot was sticking to the mud.

The Orator filled in. "I told you that Rasck scoured history. The speech we just witnessed was born and bred by the sights we are about to see." He gestured to the side and walked toward a small group of people in a corner.

Stepping with caution, Zarra followed. There was a putrid smell, and the smoky air stung her eyes. Strolling up, she saw what was originally motioned to: sick people. Black spots decorated their bodies in laughing indifference. Their skin, despite any original color, now resembled ashes. Appalled, in horror and disgust, she squeaked, "What is this?"

"Sickness, starvation, overall egregious condition of living . . . Things that Rasck has seen and judged."

Their surroundings suddenly changed, and they now stood in what appeared to be a forest. Looking up, one could see that the trees here almost touched the sky, and their trunks were so wide that no one person could come close to wrapping their arms around them. Birds fluttered from tree to tree and other assorted creatures scurried on the ground. Then, time moved forward at an expedited pace. Blurred images showed the forest being mowed down, animals now fleeing for their lives, and fire now breaking down the once-abundant life. When it was all said and done, they stood in a blackened field of ashes, and the once-clean air now was filled with particulars.

The Orator stated, "Here we see just a small example of pernicious human dominance over the environment. Remember what the Reaper said: 'We must kill so we can live, and others must die so that others may live.' Here, gifts were bought with death for those who had no idea what the price was." In his pensive eyes, one could see the flames.

\*\*\*

The two were now teleported to what the Fearnaught recognized to be "The Mirror of Men." The quietness and safety of the twinkling room proved to be the starkest of contrasts; despite this, it was hard to believe that what had just been seen was really separate from where they now were. "Think back to Manestay. Specifically, recall the first question I asked you: whether or not the day the city was destroyed appeared to be of any significance. Do you remember?" the Orator asked.

"Yes. I don't think there was anything special. I didn't see anything either."

The Orator nodded. "This is a very important observation, despite its seemingly empty meaning. It gives valuable insight into Rasck's mind."

"But . . . how?"

"Evil oftentimes likes to play upon meaning with its own version of meaning. A significant day—a meaningful one—becomes a bigger target because of the psychology behind it. However, the Reaper appeared at what we think was a meaningless time. We cannot know this for certain, but I'd agree with you that it's likely. This choice of appearance primarily shows us two things, I reason. First, it shows us that his motivation is more likely to be almost entirely internalized, something very consistent with what he has said and how he reasons. Second, it is a perfect reflection of his view of the world. He sees little meaning; it's only appropriate that he should strike on a day without any meaning. *However*, we must consider the location of where he struck: Manestay, the birthplace of the Medical Revolution. The discoveries found therein have led to more life."

"So it's almost as if he is playing on the fact with everything he said?"

"Certainly. It was a calculated attack on our perceptions and ideals, something that involved a lot of premeditation. It was a display to show the futility of life. In this example, he chose to elaborate on the fragility of our bodies and the process through which we live. We have our bodies, and he sees our bodies in his way."

Zarra suddenly had a thought. "What you said earlier . . . 'There is much more to our identities than this crude matter.' The Reaper sees the taking of our bodies as redemption, but he fails to see that our bodies are merely extensions—parts—of us."

Deceus gave a proud smirk. "Yes."

"But if we are not our bodies, then why should we care to save them? I mean, Rasck believes that killing everyone will end pain. You saw the markings upon those people . . . the starvation and destitution. We saw enormous pillars of life cut and burned down while wildlife suffered in the flames. If life is such a burden to itself, is Rasck really wrong in wanting to end it all?"

"Because of Potential, dear Fearnaught . . . because of Potential . . ." He configured for himself a chair out of the mist in the room and sat down. "I have stated again and again that many of our moral problems relate back to chance . . . or potential, as I like to say. Our physical life is a gift—something bred from a long, winding string of vicissitudes and serendipities alike. We could all just commit suicide. But what would that do to chance? For simplification, there are four entities that make up everything: physical, incorporeal, living, and nonliving. Now, to kill all of ourselves would be to diminish and, resultantly, eliminate potential in the universe. For that reason, it is not consistent with the laws of the universe. If you think about it, the Reaper is attempting to eliminate emotional and intellectual negativity by completely eradicating their chances of happening. He will never succeed, because he can only destroy our physical form, no more . . . This is, of course, a grand oversimplification. . . . But now we must finish what we started." He stood and motioned to a mirror that now appeared from the floor. In it, there was a reflection of what appeared to be a stadium. The teacher entered, and the student followed.

***

Immediately a deafening roar of voices and cheering could be heard once they entered the mirror. Like the day in Manestay, here it was also partly cloudy, and the blue of the sky was full and cheerful. In the distance, one could see green fields and pleasant hills. The Angel and Zarra floated upon a cloud just above the exposed-to-nature stadium. In it, there was a track with competitors running around it: it was a race. Zarra squinted as she saw each of the runners vying to get ahead of one another.

The Orator spoke, "Rasck is right: our bodies are far from perfect. But he fails to see that they are miracles. Look at each of them." Zarra was watching. "Look at how they move, feel the excitement! These people enhanced the potential of their bodies, taking care of them and training them throughout their entire lives for this one single race. To eliminate our bodies—to kill—or to diminish their potential would be to prevent moments as beautiful as this from happening."

At this, the leader of the race, who was well ahead of everyone else, stumbled not far from the finish line while grabbing his leg. Gasping, the crowd, already on their feet, stood stoically in awe and misbelief. The second-place runner now had a clear shot of winning. But instead of passing the fallen, he stopped, turned around, and started shouting at the other competitors to stop. To his grand amazement, and the crowds', they did, panting. The second-place runner bent down and picked up the fallen, first-place runner. However, he had just been racing and was therefore fatigued, struggling with the additional weight. As the crowd watched in silence, the third-place runner came and helped to carry the fallen. Together, the trio started walking toward the finish line. Zarra couldn't hold back a forced smile and a free laugh as the crowd redoubled into a thunderous applause once they noticed what was happening. Once the trio reached the finish line, the two carriers let the fallen down, and he hobbled over the line by himself, therefore winning the race. The other runners followed the grand, unselfish act and walked across the line together, embracing each other as they did so with smiles on their faces and sweat beading down their temples.

"Taking care of and honing our bodies creates potential. Taking care of the environment creates potential. Our emotions can be bad, but they can also be good, depending on how we choose to use them. Likewise, the world is how we choose to see it. If you only have your sights on finding the negative, it will be all you ever see; and you will miss out on seeing the underlying beauty in it all," the Orator affirmed.

# Chapter 8 – The Power Within

The couple of days that followed had no more edifying reveals behind the reinforced curtain. The time, however, served to deepen the bond between Deceus and Zarra. Though they talked little, being together created rapport and a heightened sense of purpose. For Zarra, she was learning about Soula and ideals from a historical figure. Specifically, she found the pre-Imagerion time period fascinating. "So, if you couldn't visit your imagination, how could you still experience it? How could you even know that it was there? How long did it take to build things? Wait a minute, you couldn't use Soula, but you could still feel others' feelings? How's that possible?" She had many questions. Clearly, a large disconnect existed between the two generations: pre-Imagerion and post-Imagerion. Although, Deceus was, technically, a bridge between the two.

However, as more questions were asked, it was found that there were still even more answers to be obtained; more was desired. It wasn't enough to just understand the different time periods; there was a craving to hear Deceus's past. The Fearnaught thought that the more she learned about Deceus, the better she could understand how he had become so masterful with Soula. This led to the day when she finally decided to ask him.

"How is you that you are so good? With Soula, I mean. You didn't have that long to master it before you froze yourself," she blurted out, a little disheveled at the way she asked. They were walking through a town that appeared to have been vacated before Rasck or the Falling Sun reached them.

"Hmm?" He snapped out of his concentration. The question was heard; the reasoning was wanted. Although his initial guess was very likely.

"Well, I've been thinking about our end goal. We are going to have to overpower Rasck eventually, won't we? Assuming he doesn't stop . . . and I know that you have convinced people to stop before . . . but what if the worst happens? What if we just need a little more time? It'd be best to be completely prepared in all capacities. Right?" Only the sound of their footsteps followed, so she took it as an allowance to continue. "We've seen the Reaper and know what he is capable of. But I've seen you, and you're kinda close to him."

"Only kinda close? Not even close enough?" He exhaled in humor.

"You know what I mean. What's your secret?"

"I have no secret. But I will spell something out for you." Without even making any distinguishable effort, a nearby building came apart and rebuilt itself to spell the word "Positivity."

Zarra glared at the big lettering as they strolled by. "It was *just* that?"

Deceus responded with a clear voice. "We each have our own paths to walk, mountains to climb, and seas to swim, Fearnaught Zarra. Your way ultimately will be different from mine, and I cannot in good conscience tell you exactly what you must do, though I have a few ideas. I will say this: positivity wins over negativity. For me, my path to learning and mastering the art of Soula came from simply believing that I could. Growing up, I was not adept at much. Only through effort and harnessing the power within myself did I become the force I am today. The trifecta—beliefs, emotions, and effort—play their parts, but ultimately it is how you decide to think about them that determines whether or not you get the desired influence out of them." He paused. "You must also focus on yourself. When I was very little, I had a teacher who once told me that I wouldn't become anything special."

"Really?"

"Oh yes. . . . He told me to not fantasize about doing anything important because it would never happen. Had I listened to him, and many others, I wouldn't have done what I did in the past. And, I wouldn't be in a position now to better influence the future."

"There were many others?"

"Of course." He smiled. "In my youth, I was seen as being 'too serious' and 'too critical.' It was hard for me to relate to others my age because I always had my mind on ideas. Repeatedly I was told to relax myself and not be as driven. Being somewhat stubborn but also well-intentioned, I took their words into consideration but ultimately went my own way. The thing is, I realized that what I truly wanted was something not many people understood. I didn't yet know how to get what I wanted, but I had inspiration. . . . 'Why' is perhaps the most powerful question we can ask, Zarra. Never forget that."

Zarra couldn't help but appreciate the dialogue. Too often, it is forgotten that people of influence and power and persuasion have pasts. "So . . . I should ask myself why I want to get better?"

"That and believing you can grow stronger would be wise. But you already know the answer."

"To stop Rasck."

"Now ask 'why' again."

"Why I want to stop to him? Because it's the right thing to do."

"Why?"

"Why what?"

"Why is it the right thing to do?"

"Because he will kill everyone if no one stops him."

"And why does that matter? Many people have beliefs and never challenge them. Similarly, people have emotions but never decide to understand them. Others will put in great amounts of effort toward a thing without considering why they are. If you want to become more powerful with Soula and master the trifecta, you must reason back as far as you can with each. But again, I cannot tell you exactly what this will look like. It's a maze only you can solve for yourself." Here, a moment was given. "Consider, why didn't I make sure to mention this earlier?" Again, another moment of just walking. "There are many ways to do things, not all of them completely wrong or correct—the timing neither here nor there."

"I understand. . . ." With this said, the two walked on. Zarra spent time deciphering what she had heard and customized a plan of development for herself. Then, more questions came. "Does power always have to be so . . . individual? The Fearnaughts have always fought in groups. We've found that creating camaraderie between us makes us more powerful as a unit."

"A good and true observation."

"So, if we were to . . . *stop* the Falling Sun, would that weaken Rasck? They have his protection, so it is difficult, but do they strengthen each other?"

"I'm afraid not. While groups *can* help, the power always lies within the individual. With or without the Falling Sun, the Reaper is not affected, as his power is contingent only on himself. Their sole purpose is to give him more geographical coverage so that no one can escape."

Zarra took some scrap metal lying nearby and began to toy with it, using her Soula to mold different shapes. "I've also been thinking, just out of curiosity . . . why would anyone join the Reaper? Who would want to share that mission?"

"Hmm . . . I should know better than most that persuasion is an unworldly power. . . . In essence, they are recruited by the Reaper when he senses someone who has sympathy for his cause. Indoctrination is performed for those who are selected. Some do volunteer, I have seen. But, we must be cognizant of the fact that there are people in the world who are so convinced or trapped that they see vice as the means to their way. No doubt, some of these poor souls have been so confounded by the world around them that salvation lies in destruction. For the hopeless, sometimes the way out is to remove all hope; at least then, they reason, their misery and pain will be over. And what better way to get their revenge on the world than by helping to cause its downfall?"

Zarra nodded in affirmation. "That's what I was thinking."

Deceus looked up into the sky; it was a slightly overcast day. The rays of the Sun were just poking through and were slightly distorting the imagery, making it seem as though someone had just thrown water into the sky in an effort to dilute the sharp edges. "You should know that I am largely self-taught."

"You had no teacher?"

"I had many lessons embodied in people I have met, places I have been, and experiences I have had. Ultimately, we each are the teacher in deciphering the lessons before us. You just asked me how to become more powerful with Soula. Right before you shines yet another answer. You just need to be mindful of it." He motioned to Zarra's floating metal mess that she had been playing with.

She looked at it with indifference. "So what? Lots of people play with objects to pass the time; it's nothing special."

Deceus stopped walking and feigned appearing taken aback. "Is it not?" He smiled and had a mischievous look in his eyes as they looked up. "Clouds are lovely, aren't they?" The pavement underneath him suddenly separated from the ground and lifted him up to a nearby rooftop. Raising his hands to the heavens above, he clenched his fingers as though he was grabbing something. Metal clashed against the ground as the sight of clouds being sucked down to the Angel broke Zarra's concentration. A twister formed at Deceus's fingertips that spiraled up into the swirling sky above. Without warning, giant, cloudlike creatures swam out of the tornado and proceeded to fly freely and happily, the Sun just kissing each with what little rays penetrated through the gray mass above. The largest of the creatures, in the shape of a whale, dove down and swam through the air just above Zarra's head as all of the others followed suit, flying in a V formation. Around and around they went, going faster and faster until Deceus called them back into the twister and released it to return to its natural state. From the rooftops, the Orator yelled, "Creativity! It was right before you in the shape of twisting metal—a flickering ember that has yet to be fueled into an inferno! Positivity can help, understanding why can help, and being creative can help, as can others," he rang out while flying back down to ground level. "Our conversation was just erratic, going from one topic to the next. Focus is needed, as life is chaos! Without being able to home in on what's important, it will likely just slip by right before your eyes. Let's begin again, shall we?"

"Y-yes," the Fearnaught stuttered, attempting to mirror this new energy.

"If you wish to become more powerful with Soula, you need to be positive and believe that you can. You must ask yourself 'why' whenever you can. Creativity is also an asset, especially when you are faced with an adversary with whom you are equally matched. Throwing them off guard with your creativity can prohibit their focus. Like I just said: life is chaos. Show them chaos in whatever form, be that of flying creatures born from the clouds or a manipulated environment to break equilibrium."

"And all of that should be done through myself and my own direction."

Deceus nodded. "And there is one more piece of advice I can give . . . for your consideration." He walked over and sat next to a well-decorated establishment full of many flowers and small trees. The combination of man-made and natural materials seemed so seamless that it was hard to differentiate the two. "With Soula, we cannot manipulate other living things *except* plants. Haven't you ever wondered why that is?"

She thought for a moment before responding with an illuminated expression. "No . . . I guess not. I just accepted it."

"Well, if you just would ask 'why,' you will find that one can harness the power of Soula in plants, if needed. It requires dedication and connection, but it can be done."

"Is that why we are always near or in nature? You're seeping power from wildlife?"

"I am building a more established connection, yes. This deviation from the normal powers should be capitalized on, of course. If you too do the same, wherever life is, it can back you if you call upon it for a purpose agreeable to it. That is, obviously, depending on how you choose to interact with and think about it."

Zarra shook her head in wonder. "Life is so weird."

Deceus got up, and they continued walking. "You must know by now that there are hardly any absolutes. 'Life is weird' may just be one of them."

# Chapter 9 – The First Emotion

"Just days ago, you asked me how to become more powerful with Soula. Your consideration, though various, was based primarily on safety. . . . Do you fear much, Zarra?" the Orator asked.

"Of course I do," she replied, thinking about her own musings from not long ago and feeling somewhat ashamed of herself.

"Many do. Before Imagerion, many thought that fear was the greatest motivator—an instrument. Even more today, I think, would agree. There are numerous forms, but perhaps it can be reasoned that the original stemmed from the need for safety. And this is bred from more than physical safety—certainty versus uncertainty, socialization, and expectation also, among others. The Reaper knows this, and so that is what he focused on when he destroyed Allelse, the city in which the Treaty of Allelse was signed, axiomatically. What do you know of the treaty?"

"It ended a long period of raging strife between two nations that had historically feuded for decades. Both war parties were entering mutual destruction, and it took many, many deaths for the two to realize that their war only served a terrible purpose." Zarra took a breath. "It was sick what they did. Generations and generations of kids were bred to hate one another to fuel the propaganda. Both sides claimed that it was for safety, and they were indoctrinated with the belief that they were explicitly correct in each and every way. I do . . . I do remember. The kids were eager to fulfill their parts—to kill the others. And that's all they thought growing up; there are only two sides: mine and theirs."

The Orator nodded. "When confronted with such dramatic conflict, little resistance remains for moral defense: people's minds get channeled into pernicious funnels of thought. We forget that there is no one true opposition, that their side likely has people more agreeable to us than some of those on our side, but we are blinded their location relative to that line, whether by circumstance or decision. The same applies to other forms of fear as well. People are afraid of negative possibilities and will conjure up rationalities to escape the tension."

"What do you mean?"

"I mean that a man may not pursue his dreams because of the implications it could impose. A woman may not try to escape her fate, so to speak, because of her reasoning that it is meant to be. Those who are wrongfully imprisoned, whether by bars or society, could choose to bear the chains rather than break them because they learn to love the metal. Subjugated people could cower and submit rather than rise up and endure the chaos of unfamiliarity. Do not be mistaken: fear is not so much a motivator as it is an inhibitor. The Reaper knows this and capitalizes on it. You said so yourself! His image is infectious, as is the stigma of that cloaked atmosphere. When people fear him, additional strength is granted to the Scythe. For this, we will see now a version of him much more aggressive than the previous." The two were again sitting with the Sun setting in the distance, the orange and bloodred clouds hovering over the horizon. Deceus held out his Locket and, with the connection of the other, both were teleported to another world: the memory of Allelse.

***

What Zarra saw was the Allelse she saw before, though not in person. It was a city built in the sand, a desert. Though the landscape surrounding the city was not entirely barren, it was still deprived of green. Gusts kicked up the dry dirt across the ground as Deceus and Zarra descended onto a tall building near the center of the city. The Fearnaught had learned to observe and study, to experience the onslaught through curious, though fearful, eyes. The crowds below were already in a panic, for the man on the Stone Throne had risen over the horizon. Although, this time, he had a companion. It was learned that the first of the Falling Sun was a volunteer who sought out Rasck and asked to take part in his vision. That man, named Zark, was the one who now floated into the city with him.

All around, debris was flying toward Rasck and Zark, attacks from the people below. The forces between the opposing Soula could clearly be seen where they were meeting; the Reaper's easily disposing the opposition. Together, some of the citizens attempted a coordinated maneuver to topple a tall building onto the aggressors. This was seen through the red visor, and instead of fulfilling his curiosity to see if they could do it, he simply ripped the tower out of the ground and tossed it to the outskirts of the city, where its impact formed a crater and a brief rainfall of sand. Seeing this, many attempted to now flee. Those who tried soon found that any transportation they could muster was quickly impeded from movement. Some, then, resorted to an old-fashioned method of transportation: running. The Stone Throne and its champion plus follower descended into a large crossing in the city where Deceus and Zarra followed.

Some petrified citizens stood nearby to watch what was to come while everyone else attempted to escape. Even so, there were some indecent attempts at the Reaper's life that were lazily subdued as they neared their intended target. Clearly, he allowed it to get so close only for show. With this, Zark turned to his commander. "This dread that I feel . . . it was here before even we were."

The Reaper, paying minimal attention, sat with feigned disinterest with the environs and lazy posture, Mercy in hand. Even with all of the commotion, he seemed unwavering in his demeanor. That was, at least, until he sat upright and answered by saying, "Yes, it was," and got out of his chair. The Angel and Fearnaught observed him walking back and forth, the tall buildings like walls to the heavens as the backdrop. At length, he constructed out of the nearby materials a giant square and held it up to the sky, blocking out the Sun. The object then fell and landed in the shape of a hollow cube around them, periodic holes spread through the ceiling permitting some light to come through. Though, the interior was dark and brimmed with dread. He began to address those who were in the darkness with him while the screams and panic ensued, muffled through the walls.

"Fear . . . It is intelligent, making its home in vessels recognizable to us." Holding his arms out to the side, he asked, "Do you see my attire? People conjured up a being who looked like this to better symbolize fear. . . . Though the symbol they made was black as space, for death, and I am pure, therefore bright. You see, our ancestors liked to use light to better portray what was good, whereas the opposite depicted what was bad. I question that, and I hate it for how original and shortsighted it is. But still, here we are, in a form of fear very familiar—so familiar, even, that it occurs every day. Why, in the womb, even, it is all we are surrounded by. . . . See, I like to think of fear and what it does for us—the grand motivator. And, it does not take much intellectual prowess to come to the conclusion that fear is bred from the need for safety, in its many forms." Here, he paused and continued to lurk around in lack of light, flashing from the occasional steps into and out of the Sun's rays permitted through the top. "That is what this city is most known for: safety." Outside, screams renewed as a building was heard collapsing. Through one of the crevices above, a tan document, spinning around as though on display, floated down. The environs made it appear as though the document was descending through mystical means in a ray of light. The paper stopped at eye level and continued rotating. The Reaper whispered, "Behold . . . the Treaty of Allelse." All around, the citizens trapped in the cube who were witnessing the scene shifted in discomfort. "The need for safety, the elimination of fear, is what brought the document to draft. But, it is a failed document, is it not? You see, we, as humans, attempt to create safety as per our desire to eliminate fear. But, safety can never be granted to us, can it? This futile treaty attempted to cease a war; instead, it simply transformed it—much like how our fear will transform from one concern to the next. Instead of battling with blood, combatants then fought with ideas, and culture, and other *sur-rep-ti-tious* methods. No longer was it a war between soldiers but between citizens. Hmm . . . seems ridiculous, doesn't it? I mean, this notion of certainty. No matter how hard we try, we can never be truly safe. Fear will follow us, slipping through our barriers and fortresses along the way. All of the little random chances and vicissitudes will always be there, mocking our efforts and laughing in our faces. To youth, it is the dark of the night, imaginary monsters that hide and bite and growl. For the older, it is fruitless attempts at peace and stability, and the ever-present looming uncertainty. And since we can never be 'safe,' we can never truly not fear, then, can we?" At this, he lifted the cube, and it separated and fell apart, causing no harm. Once again, the Sun and the city came into view for those who were previously ensnared. "Even in the light, you fear. Only now, your fear is more certain and can be seen much more clearly. . . . Funny how that is." The Reaper then gave a shrill laugh, Mercy glimmering in the light. "You hear me? Ah, how disorganized. That's how fast my mind is." He then paused, clearly entertaining himself with his monologue.

He brought his attention to a lady shivering with fright and staring with wide eyes. Walking toward her, she could not move; petrification had eradicated motivation and the ability for mobility. "My, my . . . my dear. You look so cold! And in these oppressive rays! Perhaps an answer could heat you up. Tell me, please . . ."

"Te-tell you what?"

"The only question I ask of you, of course. Why do you live?"

The woman answered readily, "I do because . . . what's the alternative?"

At this, the sky and everything in sight tinted red. The Reaper then proclaimed, with Mercy in hand, "The alternative is the solution. Then, we will have beaten fear, and no longer would we need to be afraid." He then turned and slashed the Treaty of Allelse in half.

***

In "The Mirror of Men," Deceus and Zarra now found themselves reflecting. The Fearnaught sat down on a cloud of mist and stared at the blue-tiled floor in rapid musing. With the galaxy in plain view above, it was a while before either of them made any initiations. "I can't tell whether or not he is right," she stated, at length; the time had stoked the conflict within.

"About?"

"The first emotion: fear. . . . I try to eliminate it but can't. Like he said, it's fluid, formless. How can it ever be conquered if its existence is intertwined with our lives?"

"Is it?" The Orator smiled and sat across from her. "Zarra, it is possible to eliminate fear and still be alive in the way we traditionally view life. Again, the Reaper thinks that our problems are solved in death and fails to see the value of life."

"Then teach me!" Her face contorted to distress. "Do you think I revel seeing what he does? I watch because I want to understand, because I want that motivation the sight brings . . . but I don't want to be afraid anymore, not of him, not of anything! You know all of these things—why can't you just transfer all that you know to me?"

The Orator waited for her heart rate and emotions to calm before speaking any further. "I have my reasons. My primary reason: many of the questions we ask have only to be answered by us through thought. The truth is, Fearnaught, I have already taught you. Fear can stem from the need for safety, but we can go further than that. In fact, if we ask 'why' and then ask 'why' some more, we will discern that the world and heavens as we know them were born of chance—potential. . . . The universe was not created from fear; it was born of chance. To use a more accurate word, our existence originated from hope. The first emotion, then, is hope—not fear. Without it, without chance or potential, all else is not possible. Look up." His gaze followed his words. Above, a purple band of stars and celestial energy shone. "It all needed a chance to exist, Zarra. Our motivations, both good and bad, all have the same underlying foundation: hope. The Reaper, in his bias, thinks that he is eliminating fear, when the reality is that he seeks to destroy all hope . . . at least in the sense we are talking." At this, a mirror presented itself out of the foggy air. Nothing could be seen through or in the smoky glass except flashes of light and vibrations.

"What will I know? What will I learn?" she whispered, peering at the mysterious beyond.

"Only what you will."

***

Through the mirror, a muddy and snowy battlefield lay in the midst of fragmented skies and riddled tree lines. Large holes were created when explosions blew apart the dirt as soldiers traversed what was formerly no-man's-land. There was no way to properly identify one side from the other; it was a pit of confusion, seemingly a single mass fighting itself. Obviously, this was a battle in which Soula was not being used, gruesome and crude as it was. As the Angel and Zarra crossed the middle of it all, through blasts and projectiles and razors alike, they looked at the war-torn faces. These people were fathers and mothers and brothers and sisters—all of them were loved. Here, however, no love was shown, only tired eyes and flashes of gritting teeth.

"Rasck hates conflict," the Orator began. "Here, we see people fighting for no good reason, not that killing can ever have a reason. Establishments far and disconnected from them commanded their presence here and provided them with weapons and a goal."

"He's not wrong to hate this."

"No, he isn't. . . . Something I had an ardent distaste for back in my time was the pride that some had for this. Weapons are bad and there is no glory in war; those who think otherwise have obviously never been there before. . . . Here, there are mangled bodies, reddened snow, and torment for the soul, which will remain in one's memories long afterward, if they survive. This battle here, however, never happened." And suddenly all that was around them reorganized itself back to its initial state. Zarra scanned the field and ascertained that it was a standoff between two opposing sides. Trenches to her left and right were filled with eyes guarding the no-man's-land with cautious interest. With this, the Angel smiled and assumed a serene standing posture with his hands together at his stomach. "Positivity wins over negativity: hope triumphs over fear." His gaze went into the distance where a soldier, presumably one of the leaders, climbed onto the would-be battleground with this hands in the air. Immediately, voices rang out on the other side and shots were fired at him. Despite a small flinch, the man was otherwise stoic and breathing easy. In this moment, an essential connection was made between him and whom he sought to speak with. Slowly reaching down, he pulled off his coat, shirt, and helmet to show that he had no offensive capabilities. Then he began to tread across the fresh snow as flakes fell and stuck to his short, cropped hair. Chattering teeth carried in the winter breeze, his pale blue eyes a lighthouse in the washed-out colors. Both sides watched in focus as one step after another brought the figure closer and closer to his destination. After what seemed like an eternity, he eventually was taken in by enemies, with Deceus and Zarra following right behind in the trenches. Through a tunnel and a series of turns, the shirtless soldier was brought to sit in a clean room with tables and maps before what appeared to be leaders of the opposition. Each sized up the blue-eyed man with extreme interest, muttering to himself. One of them, a midsize man wearing a uniform with a red collar, broke from the group and walked to the side of the room where a coat was hanging. He took it and handed it to the man, wordlessly, before sitting down opposite him.

Clearing his throat, the magnanimous officer spoke. "And what do they call you?"

"Emel," the blue-eyed officer responded, choosing to not include his rank.

The opposing officer scrunched his mouth and looked down for a second. "Very well . . . Emel . . . you crossed dangerous terrain to get here. You're lucky to not have any extra holes in you. I trust, then, that you came for a good reason?"

"A better reason than why we are here." His eyes were unflinching, subtle yet firm. Jutting his chin up, the red-collared officer waited for further explanation. Emel then continued by addressing all in the room, "I've been thinking about what we are doing here, gentlemen and gentlewomen. We are fighting, and good people are dying. And when we are not fighting, we are starving. And when we are not starving, we are freezing. In my youth, I aspired to become an officer like my father before me. Now that I have seen firsthand what we are bid to do, I renounce myself. No reason is a true reason for us to be here doing what we are doing. I, like you, have been sent for interests, but our interests are nothing if this is the means to obtain them. That is why, effective at next sunrise, I suggest that we both take our respective troops and walk away."

A couple of laughs were heard in the room. "You cannot be serious! Just walk away? A fool's errand!"

"A fool's errand?" Emel's voice was stern but without threat. "Haven't you ever considered that all of this can just stop if we just refuse to participate? Tyrants have ruled because those who administered for them, whether they be police or public servants or militants, simply did not have the courage to stop. There are ways to settle disputes; this is not one of them."

Essential moments, such as this, need a brave soul to act as the impetus. Without such acts of temporary insanity, defining moments of the human race would not come to be. The red-collared officer scratched his nose and sat back in thought. "I have had . . . similar conclusions." The other officers looked at one another in incredulity. One of them came forth. "There is no way we can even consider this! Think of the . . . repercussions. How will we be punished for this?"

"I am to understand that you have a toddler daughter awaiting you. Is this correct?" Red Collar asked the interlocutor.

The officer swallowed. "Yes, yes, but—"

"—and I am sure that you would like to see her again as the same father you were before you left? Or am I to consider our previous conversation as null?" At this, the officer slowly backed off and returned to the others. Red Collar now turned and faced Emel, looking him over for a few seconds. "It would appear to me that we are being offered a chance to rewrite history not only for ourselves but for our troops and perhaps even those whose time has yet to come. I trust that Emel would not have come in the manner he did unless he was absolutely serious, and I believe that he speaks to all of our best interests."

Emel answered, "I am."

"And though I trust you, how can I trust those on the other side? You see, I too am in charge of lives, and I will not unnecessarily jeopardize them. . . . You understand how fickle our position is. . . ."

"You may or may not trust us, but that is inconsequential, as our minds are made. Come tomorrow morning, we will toss our weapons upon the middle ground and leave the way we came."

"And go where?"

"Home. . . . And I suggest you do the same."

Red Collar scratched his chin. "You understand what it is that you are requesting of me?"

Emel's eyes flashed. "Entirely."

\*\*\*

The next morning, the winter's Sun shone over the ground, making the fresh snow sparkle. Deceus and Zarra floated above the middle ground and saw Red Collar appear in the trenches, making strides behind his troops. Opposite, one could make out the figure of Emel standing, looking over. Zarra calculated that Emel's forces were greater and better supplied than Red Collar's; leaving would be forfeiting a probable victory. And yet, Emel stood on top of the no-man's-land and dropped his weapon. Seconds later, soldiers in the trenches from his side threw their weapons up into the snow where they were gathering in clusters. Red Collar and his officers saw this, and they and their troops waited as a pair of blue eyes pierced them each, one by one. Then Emel turned, and as he walked away he heard the faint clinging of weapons from the other side being thrown upon the ground.

\*\*\*

The environment changed to what appeared to be an urban park. While standing underneath a symmetrical tree, the Angel and the

Fearnaught saw on a bench not far away an elder man. This man wore a shirt with a red collar, and he sat there to relax during a routine walk. Gleeful screams of children playing could be heard in the distance; it was a beautiful day. As the red-collared man sat there, he saw in the distance another man walking toward him with a young girl. As this man neared, Red Collar saw that he possessed distinct pale blue eyes. For a fleeting moment their gazes met, and each recognized the other; it was the first time they had met since that day they had both walked away. No words were spoken, but both gave a small nod and smile of acknowledgment as Emel walked by. The exchange lasted only seconds. The meaning, however, would last forever.

The Angel turned to Zarra.

She felt his gaze on her skin and answered, "It was not fear that drove Emel across no-man's-land; it was hope."

The Angel took a deep breath and exhale of appreciation. "It takes strength to overcome one's enemies. . . . It takes greater strength to befriend them."

# Chapter 10 – The Message

The city of Lowhi was a fairy tale to those who could see it. At a glance, its predominately stone buildings and stained glass windows were surrounded by fresh, rocky hills and little valleys rich with life most green, natural, and prosperous—a particular, rugged beauty. In the center of the city stood one such rocky hill; and on top of this hill lived the Tree of Live, an enormous miracle with dark bark of swirling designs. The shadow cast by the wild foliage was enough to cover many of the nearby structures, including the headquarters of the Fearnaughts. As the shade cast upon its many-colored windows, Leader Loyaira looked out her office in wonder. She was about halfway through her physical life and possessed dark skin, soft eyes, and an aura of motherliness. Her expression was always that of great musing; at least until action needed to be taken. Like a switch, she had the ability to adroitly change between two modes: contemplating and commanding. Through her the Fearnaughts were created, and it was thought by her that Lowhi would eventually be the last stand against the Reaper's Scythe and the Falling Sun.

A Fearnaught entered the room with haste. "Leader Loyaira, there is something you will want to see."

"What is it?" she answered, recognizing the voice.

"A meteorite has fallen not far—the west hills."

"Is that all?"

"There is writing on it about someone who can defeat Rasck."

Loyaira now turned away from the window. "What do you mean?"

"I would have had it brought it here, but there are scores of crowds near it. Word got out very quickly and—"

"Let us not waste time. If what you say is true, I must see it now," she resounded, and walked onto the balcony, where a metal horse stood. Mounting the horse, which she manipulated with Soula for transportation, she soared into the air, her guide leading the way.

\*\*\*

Just as the informant stated, there were many people who had made the short journey to view the spectacle. Objects of transportation spotted the hillside, each in accordance with its rider's style. After dismounting onto the grass, Loyaira strode through the crowd with eyes on her. The Fearnaughts, it should be said, were not entirely approved of. They were a band of vigilantes to many but were allowed to exist solely to defend against he who struck against humanity. Who, in good consideration, would deny them such endeavors?

Squeezing through the pond of bodies, Loyaira saw it: the meteorite. Dark gray and black in color, porous in texture, it sat there nicely as if posing. Carved into it was writing that read "From the

94

West, a Beast has risen. Two have fallen, three yet remain. From the Third, one will endure—The Promised. At the Fourth, the One must stand and make the End. Then, those who Fall will cease."

As she was studying the extraterrestrial material another woman stepped forth, who evidently arrived just after her, donning the garbs of an authority from the city. "This matter should not concern you, Loyaira, just as it should not concern anyone else here."

"Nice to see you too," the Fearnaught commander politically replied, noticing the newcomer.

"I have been instructed to take this back for the *officials* to review. No need for anyone to develop any . . . brash ideas." With her she brought two others, who placed the meteorite into some container by using Soula to lift it and carry it off.

"Of course, of course—we mustn't interfere. I'm sure we would all love to hear what the *officials* devise." The initiator gave a sneer of malice in response and left to wave away the citizens gathered there.

The guide who had accompanied Loyaira quietly addressed the situation. "If I am not too bold, I'd like to share my opinion. I think that our boundaries need to be expanded."

"Agreed, but not causing division among us is the trick," Loyaira confirmed. "The public will know what it meant."

"A survivor from Venestag, 'The Promised,' will defeat Rasck and the Falling Sun at Sumeq?"

"The third and fourth cities, yes."

"It means that the Reaper will not reach Lowhi after all."

"You believe it to be true?"

"With everything that has happened, it is a better alternative. . . ."

Loyaira thought while they walked back to their transportation, blending in with the crowd. "I cannot believe it to be true. It seems too well-defined and sudden . . . and who could have sent it? We will act as we always do, minus one exception."

"The exception being?"

"Bring Leonis to me as soon as we get back. I need to speak to him."

***

Upon their return, Leader Loyaira closed herself in her office—something she rarely did—and waited. To think, she had to move. So she ventured around the room and played with the various objects within, turning them over as she turned her mind. Laconic speech and an air of mystery surrounded the woman. Yet, she was entrusted with managing and leading due to her justice-craving nature and evil-punishing zeal. Placing her hand on the old, dark furnishings, she felt the texture upon her skin as the main door opened. The confidence the figure brought into the room by virtue of himself was outstanding. "You called?" Leonis half asked, half stated as he came into full view.

"Good afternoon, Leonis. How are things?"

"Oh, stop it. No need for small talk. Let's get to it, shall we? The message—"

"You know of the meteorite?"

Leonis snorted as he sat down across from the main desk. "Half the population knows of it."

"And of course, you would never be an exception for something like that," the Leader stated as she sat down behind the desk.

"Course not."

"Well then . . . I will get right to it. You know what the message stated—what it meant?"

Leonis rolled his eyes. "I'll go."

"I was afraid of that. . . . There is a reason we randomly pick who gets sent with each outing. It's so that everyone has an equal chance to go and that no one can point the finger for blame. You, on the other hand, would be going *directly* without that safeguard. . . . I don't like the idea of letting someone go to what may be their death when they were not picked."

"Save yourself the mental headache; we both know that I wasn't picked but am planning on going regardless. I've beaten members of the Falling Sun before, so I stand the best chance. If this does amount to something, I should be there."

"Yes, but those whom you did beat were far from Rasck, and here you will be meeting with the Reaper directly. . . . You are the most skilled Fearnaught, Leonis. Just make sure to not risk your life for what may be a lie."

His eyes widened for a second. "Oh, so you don't believe it?"

"I need to continue to act as though we are cornered. We— any of us—cannot afford to relinquish our belief to something beyond control."

Leonis shifted his position. "So, you aren't going to stop me from going? Even though I wasn't picked?"

"The way I see it, I have no right to dictate whether you can or cannot go. You volunteered to become a Fearnaught and may do as you please. If this prophecy, if it can even be called that, is true, I'm not sure how much bearing we can have on it."

"So you called me in to just say that you wish I would stay but aren't going to prohibit me from going?" He chuckled.

"That's right."

The outward-bound Fearnaught stood, clasping his hands together in surprise. "I'll take charge, of course. In fact, I'll ask the group to leave in two days. I have a few . . . *creative* ideas that I'd like to plan out." As he neared the door, he looked back. "I'll keep my eyes open."

Leader Loyaira gave an understanding nod in response.

# Chapter 11 – Zarra's Effort

Since their conversation about gaining strength and becoming more masterful in the use of Soula, Zarra had begun a series of independent training. Throughout the day, as she and Deceus traveled, her mind operated ceaselessly to one end: improvement. In the beginning, she had a general calling that drove her to the Fearnaughts. There, she found purpose through others. Now, however, she found purpose through herself. To start, she began to believe. In what, one may ask? One thing in particular: herself. In the beginning, she acted confused and afraid. Now she cast away that confusion as she found direction, her compass. First fearful, she now was hopeful. In herself, belief and serenity and controlled anger went. Even with the energy raging within, she found peace; the dichotomy bred focus and the ingredients for her transformation.

Every day, all day, it was the same: I can. The only failure could be found in lack of positive belief or absence of effort. So long as the will remained, the win was within reach.

When she was walking, she observed all life and made a connection to it. Through her beliefs, emotions, and effort, she began to feel the breath of the winds with a new vigor. As each exhale of the world passed by her, it could be heard whispering wisdom in her ears. Every blade of grass and speck of sand could be felt and counted as though each were an individual unto itself. The wildlife which would cross her path would not hide or cower but would gift onto her the acknowledgment and conscious pride of her pursuit.

When she was at rest, mental constructs—her imagination—would place her under thunderous waterfalls with defined rainbows in the distance and solid rock beneath her feet. Onto her water fell without leaving any marks but kisses and blessings. From the top of snowcapped mountains she could see far and wide the world—her home—and know it infinitely better. An avalanche of snow on which she'd ride would quickly turn to sand as she found herself in a peaceful desert where the Sun was not hot, but enriching. Geysers would fire into the air with the passing of the adventuring soul and fall in speckles of shimmering light. From the desert, great reefs would manifest from the barren soil, and the sky would fall into the plains as salty ocean water. In the tranquility of the deep blue, the rolling waves above and the dark abyss below, there was no panic but fierceness. From her body, heat would emit and the water would turn into clouds: suddenly she found herself soaring above her fair planet. A connection to the universe was being made as was a sense of oneness with her universe and herself. Uncertainty became certainty—the finite, the infinite.

All of this gave her a crown of focus. No longer was the extraneous overwhelming and the esoteric unknown; the key had entered the lock. Within, immaterial treasure was being found.

Through this metamorphosis, she had also exhibited creativity and a heightened sense of imagination. The detail that one could acquire through Soula paralleled the experience of life; dreams sleep on the hope they would be so remarkable and vivid. In this vacuum that was her mental state, artificial enemies and enablers of vice lashed out against her in an urban oasis. In defense, she combated them not with brute force but through calculated, artistic dexterity. Digging her fingers through the ground, she felt the power surge down her arms, causing an earthquake. Forcing them to take to the skies, she now lowered the clouds to take away their sight. With no pedestrians around, buildings could be manipulated without constraint. She used them to construct a floating maze around her adversaries to promote even more confusion. It was good practice. In another thought, she was locked in a battle of willpower against someone who was an equal match. When confronted against an equal, many times the sought-after advantage is found through effort. Having exhausted her reasoning, her emotions, and effort, according to her self-devised scenario, a new tactic was needed. In her enemy's eyes, she could see negativity. There was anger, but it was the ancient kind—the kind that drives ignobleness. Seeing this, the wanted counter was now found. She put emphasis on a particular memory: a happy one. Focusing on that, her enemy's intent to cause harm proved too weak of a force and crumbled onto itself, enabling her to successfully capture them.

From start to present, Zarra grew in the force of Soula. But even more than that, she grew as a person. While she and Deceus discovered more and more about the Reaper, the time passed, day by day. Soon, Deceus predicted, the two would be able to see Rasck before he became the Reaper. Little by little, the chance to see the face behind the mask was increasing. However, there was a problem: all of the information that Deceus had gathered via his Locket would soon cease to be up-to-date. The eradication of future cities, times when Rasck had a tendency to release pertinent information, would not be retrievable; this is because they did not occur at the initial intake. To counter this problem, Deceus told Zarra that he believed the best way to obtain more information would be to use Soula to take the Locket and fixate the mirror on Rasck when he would approach a major city (he was soon to "cleanse" Venestag). The Locket could then be used to extract the information safely. And, since the Locket was not a living thing, it would not be affected by the blast. It, however, had to be kept in mind that Rasck could feel the information being taken from him. So, it was reasoned, if his mind was harvested just before the blast, he would then rationalize that he would not need to worry about it again, since he would have cleansed the city. So long as there were no survivors, Rasck would not have to be concerned about someone running off knowing more about him than he would like.

# Chapter 12 – Our Ways

The time had come for Venestag to meet the Scythe. Deceus and Zarra waited at a safe distance at the top of a tree while the former guided the Locket through the air, concentrating with the upmost intensity. His eyes were closed and his breathing was barely perceptible. Around them, the day had just begun and was quiet as morning. After the Sun had moved quite near the center of the sky above, Deceus opened his hand in a beckoning gesture, and the Locket, which was far away, came whistling back into his outstretched palm. "This won't take long," he said, and they floated back down to the ground. After all, Zarra, with her practice, was now able to withstand more of the protection that Rasck gave to his mind.

Retreating to a large, nearby town, not too long after, the Locket was ready to be read. "It appears as though your Fearnaughts are continuing to put up a fight. This time was the best display I've witnessed thus far from them."

"Let me see," Zarra replied, determined to see some progress being made. The two both took hold of the golden-greenish metal and cast themselves into what experiences awaited them.

***

Venestag was the city of a particular type of Industrial Revolution. Here, fortunes were made, and creation brought forth entities of use. It was a perfect blend between the old and new; every old building was refurbished to be state-of-the-art. As such, it was a place of hybrid design and permitted for the ingenuity of human practicality to flourish. Throughout its stages of history, which were exemplified by historians as something of a model of previous progress, it stayed relatively the same on the surface. The buildings were large and rectangular to occupy what thrived therein; though they changed, their shape rarely did. Lands adjacent to the bustling enterprise were stripped for their copious amounts of valuable materials. It was over these adulterated lands that Deceus and Zarra, who were floating in the sky, saw Rasck and the Falling Sun rising in the distance. Here, however, there was no one to be seen to meet them. Unlike cities before, mass panic and rapid displays of desperate defense were absent. *Where is everyone?* Zarra wondered as she saw the figures approaching at a steady pace.

Unexpectedly, a faint noise could be heard growing louder over time. Searching for the source, she gazed upward to see a rainfall of large, various debris shooting down toward those clothed in bloodred. Explosions were set off below just before the man-made rains made their impact. Suddenly men and women appeared from their hiding places from above, below, and all around. It was as if the entire population manifested in the air in an awoken fury. Through their collective power, a complex series of dividers formed throughout their adversary's ranks to divide them from one another, though it was difficult to see due to the heavy smoke and traffic. But, before the people could strike at each individual, everyone was cast into cases of stone and frozen in place. As visibility increased, the Reaper could be seen standing on his throne in apparent indignation—the source of the new order. Through all of the people's efforts, only a few of the Falling Sun were defeated in the struggle, while the rest stood harm-free.

Four large projectiles, along with several smaller ones, were shot off from places unknown. Rasck blocked them with ease, but as soon as they were destroyed, mists from the inside of the casings, probably biological weapons, raced toward him. These mists too were restricted from reaching the Reaper, and he now raised his head to see several more Fearnaughts entering the fray.

Zarra looked at each of them but noticed one in particular. "Leonis!" she shouted as the lead Fearnaught sliced through the air with the second wave and broke people out of their stone prisons. With a grin full of temerity, Leonis made several passes at the Reaper using a spear made of Soula, while the second wave proved successful, and the Falling Sun's numbers dwindled. Mercy blocked each of the spears that jabbed at its master with its own brand of power. Then it orbited around its master with immaculate speed and knocked down most with its spiraling force field. Parrying this, Leonis engaged the Reaper head-on, and the two opposing Soula forces pushed against each other. "ENOUGH!" Rasck vehemently shouted. "I've had my fill of en-*ter*-tainment!" Everyone, including Leonis, was blown away by another pulse. On the ground, the people who sought to cease the Falling Sun now found their limbs covered in what appeared to be an immovable concoction of the ground. "A fantastic display! Well done! Truly, I congratulate you," the white-clad man chimed in as he walked among the trapped bodies. Efforts were still made to defeat the Reaper but now did not have the previous momentum; as such, none proved threatening. "How heroic . . . how . . . presumptuous . . . and insolent! Why, consider for a moment what this all—"

"We don't even have a word to describe you!" someone yelled, half cackling.

"Who said that?" Rasck asked, feeling incensed for being interrupted in such a style.

The answer, "I did," was heard behind him. Turning, he saw a man donning the uniform of the Fearnaughts: Leonis.

"Ah, you. Yes, I remember you. You attempted strikes against me."

"I'd call you something, but anything at all would be a step up from you," Leonis sneered, flashing teeth of defiance. "You won't win. You'll get so close, and just when you're about to taste that sweet, sweet victory, you'll lose. Wanna know why?"

With the wave of Mercy, Leonis's mouth was covered by some of the debris to prevent him from speaking further. Soon after, everyone's mouths were silenced in a similar manner to prevent them from talking.

"Now then . . . as I was saying," Rasck resumed. "Let's consider the city of Venestag." He began to pace with fervent distaste over and around the silent bodies on the ground, as though he were walking among corpses. Around him, the smoke and ashes from the conflict hung heavy in the air and greatly distorted visibility, despite the morning rays. Out of the haze, Zark appeared to stand by his commander as Rasck went on. "Within these walls the gears of free enterprise cranked, churning out products and cures and enhancements and entertainment. It all is thought to be good. But what was the purpose? Even with the power of industry and human greed behind you, nothing can save you from me and what I represent. So, I ask again: What purpose did it all serve? To enhance lives as they live? A funny thing, that is. . . . We choose to enhance lives at the cost of them! To earn a living, one must first sacrifice their life! We all remember our history, don't we? The worker works and the time twinkles on by, slowly, as lines draw across their face and gravity takes its constant toll. Hands, once smooth and free of blemish, become scarred, and wrists, once supple, become rigid and hurtful. Knees and backs ache with the strain of burden and stress.

Enhance our lives, they say! Your materialistic ways have done nothing but destroy the planet and allow domination for one over another. This culture, person, entity, or what have you is good because they work and materialize! But this one, who decides to live, is not. Says a lot about what is *incentivized*. . . . Why, it appears as though those who do the least amount of living are actually the ones who get to live! Do you see the paradox? And consider, what effect does it have on our ways—our culture? People no longer become people: they become skills and assets to be exploited. And if money is truly the harbinger of evil, then why do we base our lives on it? Our systems are pernicious and degenerative onto themselves. Futile, futile ways are ours. And what of society? Does this then not make men and women more unequal? Are our monetary systems not zero-sum games being played? Do you really think there is much difference between those of the high class and the low? Ha!" Mocking was the laugh. "Hardly a difference. There is but one true one: opportunity. In the past, peasants worked the crops as kings and queens alike ruled from their false chairs. The difference between prosperity and basic survival was based solely on the family to which one was born. To them, there was a divide, a stark dichotomy; today is no different. Like before, the wheel grinds those below. And tomorrow, the class structure will continue to perpetuate itself by metamorphosis. And opportunity can be made; but, alas, no one *can* without money and industry and resources! Why, in the back of our minds we recognize what is wrong, yet we do nothing! And when we choose to do something, we defeat ourselves. There's no trust, or support, or synergy. . . . Futile, futile are our ways; how terribly it is all intertwined!" He stopped, clenching his fists and hunching his shoulders in tension. "Anger is my weapon," he whispered, "for it is my very core." He then returned to Leonis, removed the prisoner's mouthpiece, and knelt down next to him. The sight was clear: the Reaper tended to the soon-to-be grave. "Fearnaught, what is your name?"

Only a piercing glare was given.

"Tell me, nameless . . . why do you live?"

The Fearnaught gazed straight into the red visor and declared with clarity, "To end people like you."

Everything in sight then tinted red, and the memory ended.

***

Deceus and Zarra did not immediately go back to the town in which they were. Instead, the purplish band of galaxies above and the blue hue of "The Mirror of Men" once again welcomed their presence.

"You were right about the Fearnaughts; they are getting better," Zarra started. "I noticed someone in particular."

"Leonis, you said."

"Yes. I've seen him before. He's very confident but a little brash. Still, he may have been the best of us. Leonis was very certain of himself. If positivity wins over negativity—" Zarra began to ask.

"Do not be mistaken," the Orator interjected to answer, seeing where the conversation was being steered. "Both sides of the continuum are strong. The Reaper has come close to complete mastery of the trifecta of belief, emotion, and effort. Though, he has inconsistencies—we all do. But the more I see him, the more I am brought to believe that the answer we seek is in the question."

"Question?"

"Yes, the question he always inquires."

"Why do you live?"

The Orator nodded in response as a mirror rose next to the two. "I suggest that you figure out how you would answer that question if you were ever faced with it. As an aside, I have something to show you—one of my favorites, in fact. Please, if you would." He gestured to the mirror. As Zarra stepped through, he followed.

***

Inside the mirror, the duo found themselves in a large, beige palace with gold and red embellishments and exposure to the night sky. Around them were large pillars, arches, fine linen, decorative rugs, and cozy fires that lit up the room, casting flickering shadows. Overhead, the moon was waxing among the few stars that twinkled in the darkened, deep bluish-black sky. Near the center of the room was a shockingly luxurious bed and a man with white hair clothed in a fine purple robe. Next to him, on a small table, appeared to be a half-eaten plate of food, drink, and a golden crown made of leaves. A gentle knock was heard on a door as the flames and the shadows danced.

The elderly man hoarsely commanded, "Enter," coughing as he did so. In response, the door slowly pushed open, and a boy with tan skin and black hair, perhaps in his early teens, came rolling into the room on a wheelchair. Zarra did not take long to deduce the boy was not injured and that he was born without the ability to use his legs. "You know, Entecii, when you become Sovereign, you will have to outfit the city with ramps," the current Sovereign said through coughs.

"That hopefully will not be for a long time," Entecii replied with sincere empathy.

The father shook his head. "It will happen much sooner than you would wish, I'm sure."

"Father, for what purpose did you call upon me?"

With seriousness, the reply came. "To inform you that your reign is on the horizon. Come morning, I think, you will be Sovereign." Entecii looked down, his hands slowly contemplating the wheels on his chair, and said nothing; his reaction did all of the talking. "My son," the Sovereign continued, "what do you say to that?"

"I say that I wholeheartedly do not want the title."

His father looked upon him with soft eyes. "And why do you say that, my son? Thousands of others would do anything to be in your position; it's their passion, their muse."

"Father, it's because of the people that I don't want the position."

"Explain"—he coughed again—"my son. I know not what you mean."

The fire reflected in Entecii's eyes as he thought in warmth. Throughout the room, the cackling of the fires filled the silence as the Sovereign patiently waited for an answer; he had nowhere to be, anyway. "I remember the first time Mother took me out to the fields," he began. "Ever since then I've thought about what I saw . . . how dirty the people were and how they were living. And I wondered to myself why I wasn't the same as them . . . why I got to live here in the palace with all this gold and nice clothes and people to cater to me when the others didn't. I'm not any more special than them." He looked at his shriveled legs. "I don't like the idea of having that kind of power. I'm not for it."

His father gave a weak but meaningful smile. "That is exactly why it needs to be you, my boy. Those who are capable of such leadership and refuse it for such reasons are more worthy than other contenders." His son looked at him passively. "What changes would you wish to see in our world? Speak them."

Entecii answered, "There are many, Father."

"Well, we have the night."

The soon-to-be Sovereign somewhat nervously shuffled his dark, curly hair. "I want to see the people's conditions change. I want them to be able to live more like I do and not have to work as hard so they can spend more time doing what they love. The classes . . . I dislike the structure. We should have no classes, only people and all that entails."

"And?" His father coughed.

"The government—it should be more responsive to the needs of the people; it's too slow. Plus, the guards . . . they're too rough. Most times I hear that they act before they understand; it should be the other way around. And, I want the culture to change. When I look out my window all day, I see no excitement, no happiness. I want the people to be happy, and I'd like to give them plenty of reasons to be."

"Happy?"

"Yes, happy . . . with full stomachs and lungs of laughter. But I also want to do more, for other people."

"Explain, my son."

"Father, we have power, whereas others do not. From what I've seen . . . from what I've heard . . . I think it's wrong that we continue to expand our empire. Father, I do not see the value that domination brings us—all of us. A helping hand should be extended outward for those who would grab on to it."

The Sovereign closed his eyes for a moment before opening them again with new vision. "Entecii . . . when I was your age, I had the same dreams. I failed to make them reality." His son made a move to respond but was waved off. "I let the world get to me . . . the politicians, the military, the common people . . . My greatest accomplishment, after all this time, has been raising a son who would one day fix my mistakes—you. Understand, my son, that you will be opposed, greatly, by many differing interests. Some will be genuine, others false, and others ignorant. So, you must teach them the best you can."

"Father, what would you have me do?"

"Be yourself—that boy already is more than the world deserves, and even then he will become a greater man." At these kind words, Entecii began to cry. "My son, you were born without the use of your legs. Yet, it is you who stands tall because of who you are. I pray that you never will forget that. . . . Promise me that you won't."

Entecii rolled closer and took his father's hand, looking into his fading eyes. "Father, I will never forget who I am and who you taught me to be. Even when you slowly pass on into the next, you will be in here, with me, through it all. I promise." At this, Entecii pressed his father's hand to his beating heart.

Zarra was so absorbed in the scene before her that she forgot she wasn't seeing it firsthand, and she began to cry. The Angel turned to her and shone a small, cordial, connecting smile. "Why am I crying?" she asked, almost rhetorically.

"Because you understand."

# Chapter 13 – The Foretold

Leader Loyaira waited in her office, a domicile that was familiar to internal scrutiny. The past few days were stressful, even for her. As it turned out, there was, in fact, one person who survived the cleansing of Venestag. As foretold by the recent meteorite, the third city saw one survivor, no more. And that survivor came back to Lowhi a champion—a being whom legend itself, it seemed, had created. That lone figure who emerged from the shadows unscathed was none other than Fearnaught Leonis.

Loyaira contemplated what had happened. Unlike the rest of the world, which seemed to rejoice at the news, she questioned the prophecy. It felt too perfect, too sudden. Leonis was skilled, but was it actually a voice from unknown origins that commanded this to happen? Or, was it because Leonis went for his own reasons? Loyaira disliked the negativity she was bringing—most were in elation, feeling like there now was a chance, a glimmer of hope. And who would argue that it was not to be if it was actually Leonis, perhaps the most skilled of the living Fearnaughts? After all, no protectors from any other lands or under any other names had succeeded in surviving any attack at which the Reaper himself was present.

Loyaira began to mumble to herself as a figure appeared in the room, holding its arms out wide. "Well?" Leonis said, as though he was happily asking someone what the good news was.

"Don't you think that we should have talked sooner?"

"Oh, come on. . . . I can do what I please; I'm a volunteer, after all. You said so yourself!"

Loyaira gave him a sharp look from across the room. "And what have you been doing, exactly?"

"Why . . . I've been going around and spreading the news, of course. It's good for the people—gives them something to look forward to. . . . I'm sure that you and your perfect vision have noticed."

The Fearnaught leader went and sat at her desk, while the prophecy stood. "I'm going to be open with you. Do you want to know what I think?"

"What do you think?"

"I think that you are seeking fame, Leonis, and that you are using your position right now to put on a good show for yourself. I believe that you are not fighting against the Falling Sun so much as you are fighting for yourself."

"Right . . . right . . ." Leonis's veins began to stick out. "I just decided to be here thinking that I would propel myself to fame and fortune. I just risked myself by going directly into the fray, not knowing what would happen or how. Don't you think that it's because I decided to go that I was the one who ended up living?"

"It's possible, but—"

"—but nothing! If you had demanded my presence here to just question me and later enter into some type of passive-aggressive tirade, I will go. Better things are to be done than stay here." He went to exit but was held back.

"Leonis, wait a moment! You know that I take safety seriously; I needed to ensure that you are truly fighting for the right reasons," Loyaira countered. Though, she still was suspicious of his motives and simply wanted him to stay for one particular question. "There's something I need you to consider. You have said that when you were there, the last thing you remember is everything turning a tint of red. But, afterward, you were linked with by one of the members of the Falling Sun and noticed that person lay dead next to you."

"What of it?"

"You have to think it to be . . . concerning."

The words came out as condescending. "Of course it's concerning! It was weird! But no harm was done to me, and there's no reason for any of us to be too concerned about that now. What could he have taken from me? Nothing really that would make a difference to them. Why did he do it? I can't tell you; but it was not I who killed him, that's for sure."

"And you are certain that it was not you who killed him?"

"Yes, for the thousandth time. . . . I've been asked this so much. Between you and me, I think Rasck killed him. But that's just my thought."

"Mmm . . . I see. . . . So I imagine that you will be heading to the fourth city soon? As per the meteorite's writing, of course."

"Oh yes!" His smile was back. "The City of Knowledge, Sumeq, has already prepared for my arrival . . . or so I've been told."

"Very well. Just know that you will not be in charge of coming up with a plan for the defense. . . . I'm afraid that the incursion into your mind—"

"—may have given them too much insight. Yeah, yeah, I know. Anything else? There has to be more. I respect you, so that's why I came. Respect my time now. . . ."

Loyaira refrained from talking for a moment, tapping her fingers on the desk. "All right . . . I'm still concerned—concerned about you and what will become of you. You have talent, Leonis, and you're still growing. But, I think that we sometimes find meaning in places that we should not. . . . I've been around quite a bit. I've seen what happens when people place their faith in one thing rather than another."

The foretold shook his head. "Still concerned about the meteorite, eh? Look, I appreciate it, but the matter is settled." He proceeded to leave while saying, "I'll be back," without turning around.

Now alone, Loyaira muttered to herself, "That boy only fights for himself and his own personal gain. . . ." And, of course, she was right to question and be anxious. If proved false, the prophecy would be devastating. After having the people's faith crushed that much more, the Reaper would not be met with as much opposition. And Leonis fought, while bravely and adeptly, for the wrong reasons. Those who fight for the wrong reasons, as in times of old and post-Imagerion, were at a disadvantage. However, only by letting him go to Sumeq would the foretold have a chance to be proven true; he would not be deterred from going, in any event. She just prayed that he would use his responsibility sagaciously when the time came.

# Chapter 14 – Behind the Mask

*How many can be left?* Zarra thought. With the recent downfall of Venestag, she wondered how many Fearnaughts would be present at the last two cities. The plan, according to Leader Loyaira, was to split the remaining forces—if it got to this point—to protect the last two: Sumeq and Lowhi. And, now that Leonis, perhaps their best, was gone, they would have to rely on the power of the common people and the Fearnaughts who remained. All of their deaths were sad, but she found respect for what they died for. With each wave that was sent out, Rasck's task became more difficult, slower. Without their sacrifice, it couldn't be known how far he may have now been.

*Defend Lowhi*, thought all of the Fearnaughts. It was previously worried that he, death, would reach the Tree of Live and sever the roots. Now that terrible thought was becoming clearer by the day.

But while Zarra was thinking about how many Fearnaughts were left, how the common people could stand a chance, whereas no one else could, and defending Lowhi, one other thought kept creeping into her mind. *Why do you live?* she heard again and again. Yet, despite its repetition and salience, an answer could not be devised. "Why do I live? Why does anyone live? Why are we here, and why is the world the way it is? Was there at one point nothing?

Or, was there always something? And how could anyone know?" These questions consumed her, swallowing her whole. And more than that, she again thought of what Deceus had stated to her the other day when she was crying tears of joy. "Because you understand," he had said. It was a simple phrase, but she couldn't help but think it to mean much more and encompass a scope far beyond its original context. Did she understand? And what exactly was it that she understood? Perhaps, she thought, that the answer to her questions were deep inside her; she had only to think—to shine a light—to find them.

But, at last, when all appears lost, hope shines through.

"Zarra," the Angel softly spoke. It was dusk, and the clouds above appeared as though a giant hand had swept them across the sky, like brushes of paint.

"Yes?"

"It is time to see behind the mask of the Reaper."

Her heart skipped, and her pupils dilated. She was not amazed: it had been an expectation. As such, she could only utter one word in response. "Finally."

The Angel nodded. "We will see him throughout his childhood and early adulthood. We, however, will not yet be able to see what triggered his transformation. That, unfortunately, has his greatest protection, and I will need more time to break the barrier.

But this information comes to us at a time most crucial." He held out the Locket. "When you are ready."

Zarra looked at the Locket beckoning her to see the man who fated himself to one day become the usurper of the world. Its metal spoke to her; its suspended twisting taunted her. "Do it!" it was yelling to her. "Do it!"

She took hold and felt her world change.

\*\*\*

Zarra opened her eyes and felt herself on soft, green grass with the Sun shining above. She saw only a few puffy clouds in the sky, and she heard running water from a multistoried fountain. Around her were hedges and bushes cut into geometric shapes and flowers, apparently well-attended. In the backyard of a large, white house that resided on a large estate, she and Deceus stood. "What is this?" she questioned.

"Where he grew up."

"It . . . it looks so pleasant."

"Evil comes in many forms with many pasts; no one is exempt from its influence except those who refuse it. . . . This way." Together, they walked through the well-paved grounds farther from the house.

"What's that noise? Is he hurting someone?"

"Hardly. What you hear is a game—he is playing with others."

Now coming to a clearing, they saw a field intended for gaming. All around, there were many kids. But only two were on the field playing. "I know this," Zarra stated flatly. "I used to play it all the time. Two people stand on opposite sides of a field with some moving hoops behind them. Standing in place, the two people have to use Soula to fight over the gaming orbs and get them through their opponent's hoops to score . . . and look, they even have their safety gear on." She gazed at the two kids sporting and guessed that they were probably around ten years of age. Both wore protective padding and helmets; it was impossible to see their faces. As a result, she stood there frustrated while watching the two play. However, it was hardly a fair match, as one of the competitors was much more skilled than the other. Still, it was a very strange sight to see the one who would bring the world to its knees as a little one. And to see him doing something humane and observe how popular he was, judging by the number of his friends, was shocking. "That one must be him." She nodded to the one who was clearly winning.

"It is," Deceus confirmed, and remained patient.

Not long after, the winning point was scored, and one of the kids shouted, "That's it! Iudex wins!"

"Iudex? That's his name?"

The Angel nodded, not taking his sight off the winner.

"I've never heard it before."

"It's not necessarily a name. . . . It's from a very old, almost alien-like language."

"Does . . . Does it mean anything?" She was hanging on to his every word.

"Judge."

As incredulity hit and shivers ran up her spine, the kids gathered around Iudex to congratulate him. "What the freak! How are you so good?" a voice rang out.

In response, Iudex took his helmet off and answered, "It's nothing, really—just practice, is all."

A fresh wave of an indistinguishable feeling crept up her spine. His voice, Iudex's voice, was distorted. And when she saw his face, there were no features: it was a faceless face! *"What?"* She turned to the Angel. *"What?* He's not human?"

"On the contrary," the smooth reply came, "he is extraordinarily human. And, since he is a human, he is subject to an imperfect memory. It appears that he, in all of his fury, sadness, and transformation, forgot what he looks like. Or, as I am more inclined to believe, he doesn't recognize himself anymore; that's why his face isn't showing."

"And his *voice*?"

"You can't tell me you never visited your past once?"

"Wasn't a priority of mine."

"Well, it's difficult to come up with what you sounded like when you were little. That noise you are hearing is his voice, but it sounds scratchy and . . . well . . . horrid because his memory of it is not very concrete . . . or he didn't bother devising a good replacement."

Turning their attention back to the kids, they heard one ask, "But how much practice do you do, though?"

"As much as it takes to never get it wrong. But, seriously, guys . . . it's nothing. Any one of you could do what I can if you tried more. Like, there's some strategy behind it too. Let me show you." He began giving the others instructions.

The environment quickly changed, and the two found themselves standing on a riverbed. No time was needed to see why; a short distance away they could see someone drowning. Beside them, Iudex appeared and wordlessly used Soula to command the water to bring the drowning kid to land in a wave comparable to those found at the ocean's edges. Iudex said, "Are you all right?"

Only a nod and heavy breaths and coughing were given as a response.

Iudex waited for his friend to catch his breath before speaking again. "What happened?"

"I . . . I fell in, and the current was strong."

"I figured that. I mean what went wrong? Why couldn't you power yourself out of the water?"

"Panic," the sad but honest reply came. "I was scared."

The protector knelt down. "Listen, you can't ever be scared like that. You've been told that numerous times. Your mind has to be clear, and you gotta think! You gotta believe you can! If I wasn't here to save you, think about what could've happened."

"I could've—"

Iudex nodded. "You know. Come on . . . let's get you situated." Extending his hand and pulling him up, he guided his dazed friend through the trees.

Again the environment changed, and a dining room now appeared. At the table, there were four people: a mother, a father, a sister, and Iudex. However, Iudex was now much older than he previously was, by at least eight years—he looked about twenty years old based on his figure.

"So, Iudex . . . ," the mother began. "Father told me about your decision to become a teacher. Are you sure that's the path you want to take?"

"Now, now," the father entered, "teaching is a noble and valuable profession! It is because of teachers we are where we are today. Why, with his wit, charm, and charisma, I've no doubt he will be the best there is. Think about it: hundreds of lives all touched by him."

"Oh, I don't doubt that. But he just has so much potential and can do so many things!" the mother responded. "It's just that I want to hear why he has chosen that."

Iudex began, "Well, Mom. It's just that I think I would love doing it. I mean, it'd make me feel good knowing that I am impacting the future and other people's lives; there would be community outreach and involvement . . . I've always been good at teaching too. Seems like a natural choice, really."

His sister chimed in, "I've told him he needs to do something Soula-based. He's way too good not to."

"I can do that stuff in my spare time. I wouldn't want to make it seem like a job, anyway. . . . I'll have the best of both worlds, then."

The dining room, the fine tables and chairs, and the sweet aroma of foods dissipated, and they found themselves back to where they were before entering the Locket.

"That's it?" Zarra asked. She wondered why he didn't show more.

"Just those few memories revealed much."

Without showing any affirmation, Zarra agreed. What they had seen demonstrated that Rasck once was kind, quite popular, helpful, and all-around good. Not only that, he seemed very mature, even from a young age, and had a very strong orientation toward the future. Plus, he even grew up in an extremely pleasant and nurturing environment. And to think that he was a teacher! How many people had come to know Iudex? And how abnormal it was to think that all of those people met the Reaper before he became the symbol of Death without knowing it!

Deceus didn't need to ask Zarra to know what it was that she was thinking. "The thing I favor most about what we saw," he stated, "is how it illustrates that all tyrants, dictators, and paragons of evil were once just children, just like anyone else. After all they do and after all they say, they are still human. . . . We sometimes forget that in all of our anger and frustration toward them."

"Iudex . . . Iudex . . . Judge . . . It's so weird how that works out. He literally became a judge to us all."

"It is odd. Very often, how we are thought of by others influences us greatly, if we allow it. You see, his mother had pinned him to be something very special, like all good mothers do for their young. She equated him to a younger version of a very well-known, almost ubiquitous, fictitious character. This particular character was also very talented when he was young and was promised to do wonders. However, his world turned dark, and he later would become an agent of evil. . . . I wonder whether or not his mother knew what the character would become and whether she still would have made the comparison if she knew. Iudex hated the comparison because he knew; in fact, he pledged to never become that character. While I imagine he thinks that what he is doing is far different, it is eerily similar how their timelines compare."

"So what do we do now?"

"We go forward, as always, and continue to humanize the villain."

"If we meet him, will humanizing him make a difference? I mean, it won't make him stop, will it?"

"I don't know. But, we have to try, for all of our sakes."

"He will be approaching Sumeq soon."

"I know, Zarra. I know. We must get ready." Time was running out.

# Chapter 15 – Pride and Deceit

The fourth city was approached, and in the fading, western Sun, the shadow of hollow corpses crept over the land in the form of bloodred cloaks. The Locket was already positioned to capture the moment and hung high above on the ceiling of the world. In the sky, the Locket experienced serenity. Below, fury and passion ensued in the form of mutual hatred and destruction. The stark contrast served as a reminder of a decision that we sometimes have to make. Below, there were judgments made before there was understanding. Above, removed from it all, knowledge was first sought.

This fight, unlike the others, was exhaustive. Rasck did not participate and did only two things: protected himself and observed. Like the angel of death, he oversaw the war between the common people, Fearnaughts, and Falling Sun.

The city of Sumeq was known to be a center of Enlightenment. Most noted for its prestigious libraries and museums, its most iconic structure was a large pyramid with an eye perched at the top: the Library of Eye. It was on this eye that Rasck sat while the defending combatants were pushed backward toward it, for it was at the heart. The Sun, falling in the distance, reflected in the many windows of the pyramid structure. Though the city was not burning, the fiery orange reflected in the panes made it seem so.

While there were many points of interest in the fray, perhaps the most prominent was the engagement between Zark and Leonis. Without the Reaper participating, Zark took his lead. Leonis, in his pursuit, noticed this, and the two had been dueling each other ever since. While flying objects, motionless bodies, and crumbling buildings got between them, they never lost sight of one another.

Without conscious effort, each of those who fought to survive rallied around Fearnaught Leonis. It was he who, after all, was aligned by the stars to deliver them from evil. As they began to gravitate toward him, at the base of the Library of Eye, their forces dwindled further and further. From then, it was not long until there were just a few Fearnaughts remaining and a large, circular shadow cast down on those remaining. The fighting stopped. High above, the Reaper had dislocated the Eye belonging to the Library and was now standing on it as it floated through the air, leering at them all. It descended and hovered just above the ground next to Zark, in front of Leonis, who was still breathing heavily.

"Do you want to know what is . . . interesting about our confidence, our egos? They're false," Rasck began, still on top of and commanding the Eye. "Just to show you how very fragile and vain they are, Zark devised an experiment. He came to me wishing to show the world how stupidly it believes in so-called heroes and heroines. To do so, he sent a message to you. Of course, you didn't know it was from him—the meteorite. But you all took the bait. It wasn't hard to pick which one of you should live either. Why, the one called Leonis here practically volunteered by being so bold to attack me directly. Isn't that right, Leonis?"

Internally, Leonis was racked with how easily he and the world was played. So desperate for help, they turned to something as trivial as a prophecy. Now the world would have their faith crushed when it found out that it was a clever ploy to exploit what little hope they had left.

"Thank you, Leonis," the Reaper continued, "for participating in this very important lesson. And to capitalize on the lesson, it will not even be I who discontinues you. That responsibility and honor I bestow to the deviser." He nodded to Zark, who took a step forward and shot a bolt through the defenseless Leonis. And just like that, the Promised departed. "How anticlimactic." The Reaper shook his head and spoke louder for all to hear. "How *anticlimactic*, I said! Our stories are so . . . *perfect*. Well, in case you haven't realized yet, this is far from a perfect story. Even our existence has been far from it. Look at us!" He gesticulated to everyone. "Fighting like vermin amongst the streets! We think ourselves to be separate, but the reality is that we are dependent . . . dependent on the world, our flawed knowledge . . . our misguided self-worth. You see, there's this familiar cycle that occurs. One day, we will think ourselves to be ruler over all—sacred dominions, strong castles! And then the next, we will be left in the ground to be swallowed by dirt. Kings, queens, business magnates, policy makers . . . no one is exempt. For all of our falsified power, not even those on the highest of thrones prove to be any different in the end. And in the end still, all that we have built, all of the wisdom we have gained, will crumble. Time will and time can. We all will fall; it's only a question of when, not even of how or why or where. Even the so-called best of us." He gestured to Leonis's body. "This, dear humans, is enlightenment. Take it as you will; it will make no difference in the eyes of the Reaper. Go now, the few of you that remain." He waved. "Tell those at Lowhi who has sent you and what he has decreed. And fret not, your time is soon to come. So the sands of time lessen. . . ."

The few Fearnaughts and people quickly sped off, not wanting to dispose of this rare opportunity given to them. As they were leaving, the Reaper swung Mercy into the Eye's pupil and ripped the structure apart.

Under normal circumstances, the Locket would have captured what had happened through the Reaper himself. However, without everyone being killed, there was a risk in taking memory from that original target. So, instead, the Locket extracted memory from one of those fleeing the scene. The person noticed but dared not turn around. Behind them, the Locket sped off into the distance to a beckoning, outstretched hand.

***

After Deceus and Zarra had visited the memory of the survivor and saw the previously related struggle and speech, they traversed again to the familiar, misty, mirrored room with galaxies and starlight above.

"Not a bad initiative by Zark," Zarra stated. "Planting a false prophecy to lure people to believe in one whom they would later kill. Then they made sure that survivors would go and explain what happened to bring their heightened senses crashing down to despair. . . . Not bad at all."

"You seem indifferent toward Leonis's death," the Angel observed, now taking the time to discuss an ongoing trend.

The words struck Zarra's core, vibrating. She searched for words but found none immediately, for it was true; she had been growing colder, less sensitized to the horrors. Speech then came. "Yes, but . . . I've seen so much. Should I still be horrified each time? My focus should be on our goal of stopping him."

"And that is where your focus should be. But, to answer your question: yes, you should. Even if you had seen what you saw a thousand times before, you should still feel appalled, even if the feeling is hidden by experience. . . . It's a perpetuating problem that Rasck eluded to."

The sudden, subtle change in topic took hold. "What do you mean?"

The Angel smiled. "Do you think that I say everything that I would like to about a particular thing at any given time? Do you think he says everything and points out all that he would like to?"

"Of course not. So what can we infer from what limited speech he had?"

"Let me show you," he said, and a mirror appeared through which they both entered.

***

Unlike most other mental constructs that were visited, this one was rather dull on the surface. The two found themselves in a very suave room with men and women alike dressed in dapper clothing indicative of those with positional power.

The language they were using was unfamiliar to Zarra. "What are they saying? I can't understand any of it."

"Come . . . sit with me." The Orator beckoned. Together the two sat in a corner of the room as he then explained, "These people—policy makers—are in the process of debating about a risky economical project. Their words, however, are not as important as their actions and how they carry themselves. All we need to do is watch, for now."

Zarra playfully felt the fine rug beneath her feet as she observed. Laughter intermittently filled the room with ease as did smiles and what appeared to be carelessness about the topic at hand. In essence, an understanding of what exactly was being said was not needed; their motives and self-appreciation was deducible from other factors.

After some time spent in observation, the Orator began once more after drawing a quiet breath. He leaned in toward Zarra as his gaze still followed those in the center of the room. "When you talk about ego, power should also be talked about . . . whether that be about patriotism, culture, nationalism . . . the whole lot . . . There's this giant, moving, momentous thing that we all are traveling on—most people, that is. Still, at the forward position of this thing are people like those here. Their job—or so it is said—is to keep the rest of the line in line. To do so, they conjure up a mixture of fear and hope, some propaganda, and try to essentially balance it all out so the line is uniform. And this is thought of as good because the line then is always moving forward toward progress. However, it is failed to be seen that *their* line only ever moves in circles. Their line—a very important one—may shift in and out of size and variation, but it never really changes its fundamental shape of repetition. We know how much Rasck hates all cycles in life, and how they all cause pain and whatnot. This is another example." He clapped his hands, and the two were transported with their seats to an ugly, barren landscape. Sad little huts were scattered about the lands—people's homes—and malnourished bodies littered the grounds, their skin outlined by frail bones. "The decision that was made by those policy makers far, far away did this. And yet, they will never know of it. And so, they will remain prideful because of how they are reinforced and continue to make destructive decisions."

"But why?" Zarra gasped in semi-horror as bugs swarmed the nearby bodies; they were still animate but hardly gave any effort to wipe off the eager insects.

"Because that is what is expected of them. Their job is to keep the line in line. This, right here, is the end of the line. And, notice, they are in line. You must see, it is difficult for those at the front to see so far back. Perhaps they will learn of it, perhaps not; it will make no difference to them because of the line they have inherited."

"Inherited?"

"Yes. Those who were in that room had obtained that power by playing the game. And, by playing the game, they became part of the game. No longer are they the pieces attempting to win the prize but the rules that dictate who shall win from now on. And only by following their rules, the perpetuated rules, may others get the prize. It's a sad system—our line of power," he reflected, and the two found themselves again in "The Mirror of Men"; their chairs were no longer handsomely crafted wood, but soft and supple clouds.

"Why did you show me that?"

"Zarra . . . we can beat the Reaper, but as long as these evils persist, our victory will not hold."

"But you beat the system! At New Hope City, you broke the line."

"And then I froze myself because I was partially worried that the changes wouldn't stick. I knew that New Hope City was ready, but the world? That is why I froze myself: the belief that I would be needed again. And, hopefully the next time, I thought, things would be more ideal. While I may be great at speaking and persuasion, I can only talk to those who are willing to listen. But now, it all is on the verge of extinction. Lowhi is the last major city he has yet to reach. The Tree of Live is in danger, and we must now separate. But before we do, I can now show you what made Iudex into what he is today: Rasck the Reaper."

# <u>Chapter 16 – The Reason</u>

"You know?" Zarra gasped, feeling the tension rise within her and not forgetting her aversion to being separated from her mentor.

The Angel gave a slight nod and looked up. The stars in "The Mirror of Men" reflected in his eyes as did the galaxies in his pupils. "I will show you what made him who he is today in just one scene."

"Just one?"

"One," he repeated, and a mirror appeared next to them. Together, they wordlessly entered through the reflective glass, and the rest of the mirrors that bordered the room still shone their mixture of history, feelings, discoveries, and meaning.

*** 

From the gray heavens above, the sky was crying. The tears fell hard and fast while the trees gently swayed back and forth, disposing of their leaves in the late-fall weather. Without it being overbearingly obvious, the environs were chilly and blotched with mud, dead foliage, and broken branches. As the Angel and the Fearnaught stood, feeling the tears of the planet upon their own faces and breathing in the subdued, gasping winds, beneath them, only a few paces away, lay a man facedown in the mud. Clearly, though he was dressed rather immaculately, he cared not for his clothing. Unlike his usual white, shining attire, he now wore pitch-black. One couldn't see his face, for he had it buried in his arms as the rain came down over him in sympathy. This figure wallowing in the mud, getting covered by falling leaves and dead branches, was undoubtedly Iudex. In front of him were four tombstones. One for his mother, one for his father, one for his sister, and one other. This last tombstone is the one upon which he lay while crying harder than the rain. Upon it was written one word, a name: Verity. Seeing this, Zarra needed to ask no questions nor did she have to think very hard. Beyond all doubts, before Iudex lay his deceased wife: Verity. Who Verity was, what they did together, and how she made him feel was embodied in the very manner of which she was mourned over. Iudex was here, alone, with everyone he must have loved intensely no longer with him physically. And it appeared as though Verity's grave was just added. It was in this moment of serene sadness that the Fearnaught no longer saw the Reaper as an enemy. Now she saw him with fresh eyes for what he truly was: a human who had lost all that he had loved. All that he did, and all that he said, seemingly washed away with his tears. The Reaper acted to destroy the world to ensure that no one else ever had to endure the same pain that he had to. It was not out of puerile evil, but well-intentioned good. And for these reasons, she began to cry out of empathy for him. Turning to the Angel, Deceus Stormeus Maximus, who always appeared to be imperturbable with a disposition of unwavering equanimity, she saw that he too had streaks flowing down his cheeks. Why was she crying? Why was he crying? They were crying because they understood.

# Chapter 17 – Righting Wrong

It was decided that the next day the two, Deceus and Zarra, would separate. For what and why, Zarra knew not. And while the oncoming implications of recent developments danced in her mind, she focused primarily on the Reaper and her new feelings. All of that previous heat aimed toward vengeance cooled off in an instant in yesterday's rain. To see him—Rasck—so broken and powerless gave him an element she could not describe; she only knew that she felt ashamed by how the world saw him. What if someone had reached out to Iudex at that time of inner conflict? Isn't it hypothetically possible that if she were there and knew what was happening, she—or anyone—could have prevented the Scythe from taking up arms? While it was the Reaper who sought to usurp, it seemed only fair that the world take some of the blame. Behind every villain is a truth, whether it be perceived or actual.

Today, it seemed, in an effort to mirror yesterday's journey, the sky turned gray, and sprinkling rains came down, softly and slowly. Deceus had been holding on to the Locket, in some type of mental construct, and was thinking intently as Zarra sat nearby contemplating.

At last, Deceus stopped and turned to Zarra—their eyes met. "Deceus," she began, "I've been thinking. . . . If Rasck scoured history, wouldn't that mean that he knows you? Perhaps maybe even better than most people today?"

The Angel nodded and quietly said, "He knows me, yes."

"You're going to have to meet him soon, won't you?"

"Now that I know why he turned into what he is today, yes. Waiting any longer wouldn't help anyone now."

Her eyes shifted in understanding. "What will that be like?" she half whispered. "You don't want to fight him, do you?"

"Only if I absolutely have to."

"And if you do, can you beat him?"

"Who says I need to beat him?"

Zarra looked at him in discomfort. What was said wasn't the answer she had hoped for. Even something like "I don't know" would have been more understandable. But this?

Deceus threw the Locket to Zarra; she caught it cleanly. She was about to ask him why it was being given to her when she looked down and noticed something she hadn't seen on the Locket before. On its goldish-green surface was the mark of Soula: a half circle (representing a rising Sun) on a horizontal line with three arrows coming upward out of the Sun. One of the arrows was on the top-center, while the other two were to its right and left. "The symbol of Soula . . . ," she stated in recognition. "There are three arrows for each of the trifecta. One for beliefs, the second for emotions, and a third for effort."

Deceus smiled. "It wasn't known at the time around Imagerion whether or not the Sun was rising or setting; the arrows help to make it clear."

"Why is this being given to me?"

"Instructions. You are to take the Locket to Lowhi, to your father. Once you have given him the Locket, I need you to then take it to Rasck before he attacks. I am going to go to New Hope City, just beyond Lowhi, and instruct the people there to come to Lowhi's aid. They will listen to me, after all, considering my past there."

*My father?* Zarra thought. "Why would I need to give this to my father?" She then asked aloud, "That's it? That's all you need? I . . . I'm sure that we can do more."

"There is one more thing. . . ." He stood and looked into the distance. "Right your wrongs with your family." Zarra remained silent and introspective. "You have told me that your past haunts you, as I'm sure it does with your parents. One of the most corrupting things I ever saw and continue to see is good people doing nothing while living in the shadow of vice and iniquity. They turn their eyes, hearts, and minds away and live their lives, day by day, without shining bright enough to overcome their silhouetted selves. Take advantage of this opportunity to show your true self, and in the process teach the people to act now against those who do the atrocities they do."

"Are you going to stay at New Hope City once you get everyone out?"

"I am."

"What are you planning on?"

"I am planning on you giving the Locket to Rasck, who will leave Lowhi and come to me immediately. Then, I expect you to beat the Falling Sun with the people of Lowhi, New Hope City, and the remaining Fearnaughts. Rasck will not instruct his followers to attack the city; he feels responsible for personally eradicating all life—that is why he has not taken to more extreme methods like creating earthquakes or tsunamis."

"He can do that?" she asked, apparently not knowing the true extent of the Reaper's strength.

"I believe he can, and we should be glad he feels a personal calling. If he didn't, I can imagine that those . . . *superficial* methods would have been utilized."

The Fearnaught now thought about what was needed to be done and how it could be done. How could she convince the people to ride out and fight? Would she even need to, or would the people have realized that they needed to flee and done so already? And, even if they did listen to her, how could they even defeat the Falling Sun when no one else could? Zark, who defeated Leonis, would still be there, after all.

Deceus spoke again. "When we first met, I explained to you how important it was to recognize that your actions are your own, not something beyond yourself. And we established that you would never cease until the Falling Sun and the Reaper were stopped—"

"You do not need to elaborate. I know what it is I am risking. I only wish that I knew how to be victorious. . . ."

He smiled, as if that was a comment he was waiting to hear. "But you do know, which is why I trust you to not only win but save *everyone* there."

"What?" Zarra's eyes widened as she felt the responsibility weigh on her shoulders. *"Everyone?"*

His eyes, like rays of warmth in the drizzling rain, confirmed the word without a word. Then, he spoke. "At last, Fearnaught Zarra, we must separate. You are more ready now than you have ever been. Go! Fly over the line of the Falling Sun, and they will not strike you down, for you will be heading where they too are going. . . . One last thing! Remember, Soullexes do not need to be something physical!" Beneath his feet, a transport was created in the shape of a cloud, and he turned to go.

"*Wait!*" Zarra called after him as he started to float away. "What should I do after?"

"Only what you think is the right thing to do, Zarra," he called, and soared away.

Now alone, she could feel the stress starting to seep in. All at once, everything appeared to be abrupt and surreal. Even though she wasn't moving, her heart rate began to increase, and she could feel her chest vibrating with anticipation. Now she had the responsibility and ability to directly influence whether or not people would die or live. Now all of her personal training would come into play. Now all that she had been exposed to and learned would be tested, and if she failed, it would cost life, future happiness, and opportunity. But then she remembered that this opportunity was what she had asked for, and that gave her strength. Spirited with new vigor, she felt the drizzling rain filling her with new life. She felt the improving quality of air as the cooling sensation of the water flowed over her body in tides of oneness and she put the Locket around her neck. A mirror appeared before her, and she looked into the incorporeal reflection that was her internal world.

Inside the reflection, the memory of those runners who crossed the line together and the message they gave to a roaring crowd came into her mind. Following that, the soldiers who had thrown their weapons on the ground, despite the probability of the horrid repercussions to themselves, in a commitment to a more prosperous future. Then, a teenager who would have all of the power in the world yet opted to use that power for others' benefit rang through. The sight of leaders who did not act justly and therefore cost others their ability to live finished the scroll in her mind. She then saw her past self in the mirror staring back at her with eyes full of respect for the person she had become. "I am a Fearnaught," she whispered. "I will not bow nor will I break. All that we are, I seek to protect and save. May my bravery guide me to save the lives I sought. Come, what may . . ." Beneath her, she conjured up a transport in the form of a chariot with wings and blasted off into the sky with the air tossing her hair back in a flowing posture of power.

On her way to Lowhi, the Falling Sun saw a winged chariot surge through the sky and watched it in question as it flew by.

# Chapter 18 – Fear Not

Upon Zarra's arrival in Lowhi, she could quickly see the city was in deprivation. As her chariot touched down on the aesthetically rugged but well-maintained street in front of her house, it was evident that a good portion of the city had already left. Homes appeared to be vacant—or at least very quiet—and not many people were out and about. As she walked up to the door of her parents' home, she could feel gazing eyes peering out from the other domiciles. Not needing to knock, she proceeded through the lavender door and found her father and mother inside talking quietly. With amazement, they both turned to her and simultaneously said her name, "Zarra." Together, the three shared a long-desired hug and a moment of silence. As they pulled away, they both looked her over.

"We hadn't heard from you for the longest time," her mother stated, unsure but grateful for the surprise visit.

"We feared . . . the worst," blankly stated her father, who began to smile in happy shock. "What happened? Where have you been?"

"Mom, Dad . . . I'd love to talk, but I'm here with a sense of urgency. Do you know of Deceus Stormeus Maximus? I'm sure you have. . . ."

"The speaker person? From forever ago?" her dad asked her mother.

"Yes . . . the one from up north at New Hope City. The Coliseum, the Great Storm . . . Of course! But why?" Her mother turned to Zarra, confused. Weeks ago, she had thought her daughter to be dead. Now, she stood before her as well as ever with an aura of alacrity and command, speaking of a person from the past.

"He's alive. I know because I met him and have been traveling with him for all this time that I have been away. Long story short, he plans on stopping Rasck and requested me to do some things to help him." At this, her parents sat down and looked at their daughter with an austere demeanor. "First off," Zarra continued, "he needs me to give this to you. There's likely a mental construct in it he wishes you to see." She pulled out the Locket, which was tucked into her shirt, and it hung with faint reverberation. "We will be receiving the people of New Hope City shortly, perhaps even today or tomorrow—that is where he, Deceus, now is. With the people from New Hope here, he then needs me to give this Locket to Rasck, who will fly off to meet him at New Hope City. With the Reaper gone, we then have the responsibility of beating the Falling Sun. I know—it's a lot. But you have to trust me on this."

Her parents remained silent and turned to look at each other, studying the other's reaction. After a few moments, her mother stated, "We were thinking about leaving, Zarra. In fact, most of everyone is or already has gone."

"The world has been in disarray while you've been gone," her father picked up. "Forget the Falling Sun . . . the Reaper . . . What they have done on just this continent has rippled out to others. It's all in a state of unrest, but I think our chances will be better elsewhere, not here."

It was easy to see the uncertainty and conflict of decision in her parents' eyes. Without giving it any thought, she took off the Locket and handed it to her father. As she took his hand and closed his fingers around the metal, she requested, "Tell me what you see," and then pulled away.

"You want me to link with this? It's a Locket, not a living thing. I don't think it's even possible."

"You can—it's special. Trust me," she coolly stated with a tint of joy. "It's wonderfully special."

Her father gazed at the bizarre object for a moment and then closed his eyes as he began the link. Not long after, he returned to them, smiling and chuckling.

"What was it?" the mother asked, scooting closer to him.

"Check it out with me," he offered with a voice of pride. Joining hands on the object of wonder, they both now linked with it. Like before, the journey was short and ended with both coming back with happy expressions and body language.

"What did you see?" Zarra asked with curiosity.

"The dance recital." Her father laughed. "Remember that? You forgot what you were supposed to do, and I came up to help you. You know, we both danced together in front of the crowd onstage?"

"It was crazy," her mother said with a somewhat mischievous, shy grin.

"Crazy?" he combated with playfulness. "Best standing ovation I ever got! And the only one too. . . . Why, I felt a connection with everyone in that room. Everyone was connected to one another, it was so good! You tell me of another spontaneous moment like that which got everyone smiling and applauding."

Hearing her father and mother reminisce about the moment got the Fearnaught thinking. Truly, it was one of the few times her family was ever openly appreciated. And the music was so lively, and everyone there was jiving. . . . It truly was an outstanding connection between . . . "That's it. Oh my, that's it!" she yelled in felicity.

Her parents stopped and asked, "What's it?"

"Positivity wins over negativity! The connection, the . . . the . . . I need this back." Zarra grabbed the Locket and once again put it around her neck. "I'll be back. I'll explain everything when I get back! Don't go anywhere!" she half commanded, half yelled as she sped out of the house.

Now alone, her parents again looked at each other. As quickly as exciting news came, it left.

"Dear . . . what just happened?" the husband asked the wife.

"I can't say. . . . Something wonderful, I'm sure."

***

It was in a meeting room in the Fearnaught Headquarters that Zarra found Leader Loyaira. The Fearnaught commander, who was planning with others what they were going to do in regard to the coming attack, recognized Zarra from their initial meeting. From what she remembered, she was very impressed with how certain and committed Zarra appeared to be when she asked to join. Of course, all of those who came to join were serious and driven; to stick out among the crowd required some special combination of words and demeanor. After Zarra had interrupted the meeting and told everyone there her story and what she thought the city should do, all of those in the room began questioning the proposal.

"There is an enormous risk in what you are advising," one said. "It's been considered before, but it's dangerous. It can fall apart if just one person—"

"It won't," defended Zarra.

"How could you know? Seems too susceptible to volatility," another questioned.

"It won't because it will have to stand; there is no other alternative. You could all leave now, but when else will things be as opportune? How many more will have to die and how much more will have to be destroyed until another opportunity—if *any*—is again presented? The original statement has always been to 'defend Lowhi.' Deep down, I think we've always known that it would come to this."

After more exchanges, Loyaira finally heard enough to make an informed decision. "Zarra is right," she stated. Everyone in the room stopped and acknowledged the new opinion with attention. "I think it has a strong chance to work if we can manage it." At this, Zarra felt the blood pumping through her and a fresh adrenaline rush; she was one step closer to all-around success. Everyone in the room now implicitly understood that the final decision was made. Now all they needed was a plan of action. "The thing is, the more people we have, the stronger it will be. If the people from New Hope City come, we will instruct them immediately. Those who are remaining in our city will likely join us. If they wanted to leave, they would have done so already, especially when the officials left. Let's inspire them to stay and fight with us. Spread the word that a general meeting will be held tonight underneath the Tree of Live."

"All right, let's get it done!" someone yelled, and everyone but Zarra and Leader Loyaira scrambled out the door in a hurry.

Now alone, Leader Loyaira was able to address Zarra in a more personal matter. "With this being your plan, you know that you are going to have to lead it."

"I know . . . and I will."

"Mmm . . . how much do you trust this Deceus character?"

"With all my heart and my life."

"Well, while this will likely work for the Falling Sun, I can't imagine how we could swing it with the Reaper. I hope your friend knows what he is doing."

***

Later that night, everyone who was left in Lowhi met underneath the Tree of Live. Beneath the behemoth that was dark, swirling bark and rich, green foliage, Leader Loyaira and Fearnaught Zarra spoke to the people with honesty under a starry, moonlight sky. When all was said and done, the Fearnaughts, with their bravery, inspired the common people who remained to stay and fight. The day after, scores of people from New Hope City arrived and were informed of the plan.

# Chapter 19 – Actualize

The days that followed were fabled for Lowhi. Together, the conscious choice to stay and fight gave those brave souls a breath of confidence. Upon seeing the happy faces and jocular banter, one thing became very clear—those who remained were going to fight for something other than survival. Before, every city that had fallen, in Zarra's eyes, did so out of fear. But here, hope prevailed. There was no clear reason for this either. Could it have been the great feasts full of camaraderie and rapport? Was the trust that people now had for one another and the new, neighborly bonds that were being created why? Or, was it the heightened need for one another and the increased salience of dependence on one another? Hope was enabled and promoted over fear for a variety of reasons. Overall, however, there was one thing: a specter—a grand spirit of sentient existence that made each a part of something unexplainable.

When confronted with turmoil, whether man-made or from Mother Nature, humans have a choice. Instead of looking to steal, we can be eager to share. Instead of taking up weapons, we can love. Instead of seeing others as enemies, we can see them as friends. Instead of having negative perceptions, we can learn to see in new ways. Instead of being afraid, morose, and visionless, we can have hope, zenith, and purpose.

The people and Fearnaughts of Lowhi and civilians of New Hope City made their choice.

***

At last, the day of schism came. Zarra was approached by scouts who stayed outside of the city to forewarn of the Falling Sun's presence while the rest of the city was being alerted to their coming arrival. Taking off into the sky on her winged chariot, she anxiously waited for the horde to come into view. At long last, she no longer was a ghost visiting mental constructs of city's onslaughts; she now was in one. From the west, the Falling Sun rose as a mass of crimson red. With the mostly light gray sky, their color contrasted brightly, making them more noticeable, like a disease in a place it doesn't belong in. Looking down, she noticed her parents and Loyaira looking at her from their respective places, along with many other faces she learned to recognize over the previous days. Now seeing the scourge within an approachable distance, she sped off with the memory of all of those faces flashing before her eyes, even as the Scythe shone despite the absence of the great star behind the curtain of clouds.

As she flew toward them over the hills and trees alike, the figure of a stone throne, front and center, became more and more defined. Imagine what it is like knowing that you are staring death in the face. What would you think? What would you feel? What would you do? To Zarra, even with her training and composure, it was still slightly unnerving now that it was happening. And as he, the Reaper, and she drew closer to one another, the feeling of remorse too came over her. Not personal remorse, but empathy for the man—remorse for how the world acted. Before her was someone who had become so twisted that he was unrecognizable to himself. A future once so bright and prosperous was cut short and manipulated against humankind. It was because of this that she approached him feeling no true fear but stayed composed from understanding.

Above the hilly, green landscape, both parties stopped when they were in comfortable speaking distance to one another. Many, many eyes she could not see but feel were piercing her with genuine wonder.

The Reaper spoke. "Fearnaught." Hearing his icy, articulate voice in person as he sat in his throne was surreal, considering her journey. "Have you enough sagacity to come surrender?"

"Just the opposite."

"Tell."

"My instructions were explicit. I was told to ride out to you upon your approach to the city and give you this." She unveiled the Locket. "No more and no less."

Without hesitation, the Locket was drawn from her and landed in the right hand of Rasck, as Mercy was in his left. Obviously, even though his eyes could not be seen, it was evident that he was studying the object with interest. He thought for a moment before questioning, "Who asked this of you?"

"You will find out."

"And why would I be given this?"

"I cannot say. But, you are to link with it."

Zark, who was just behind his commander to the side rode up next to the throne. "Shall I dispose of this one?" An eager, malevolent glare could be felt emanating from behind his mask. Sensing this, the rest of the Falling Sun started to incrementally advance forward, smelling the potential for blood.

"Not yet . . . not yet. I wish to see what this is. It is most *unusual*." At last, despite the growing fear that he would not link with the Locket, he now did. For several moments he did not stir. In the meantime, Zarra had to wait, vastly outnumbered, in front of many people who sought to cause her harm. The clouds slowly rolling over them was really the only indicator of the passing time. Without wasting any movement, Rasck now suddenly stood on his throne and turned it to face his army. "You will not touch a single soul in the city of Lowhi until I return. You will descend here and not advance until I return. Do *not* betray. The Tree of Live is mine."

162

The Reaper turned his look back to Zarra and stared at her so his dominance could be felt and comprehended. Then he blasted off into the sky toward the direction of New Hope City.

The Falling Sun, in obedience, descended to the ground. Zark, however, stayed airborne and yelled after Zarra as she turned to return. "Be scared, Fearnaught. Your kind is fun to kill."

Hearing this heinous callout, she could not ignore it. She adroitly swiveled around, stood straightened, and leered into Zark's face for a few seconds to establish an acceptance of the challenge. Using that silent intimidation, she then opened up the clouds to let the Sun shine through for just a moment on her adversary so he could feel the heat. What was the gesture meant to say, exactly? Perhaps it was a statement to Zark of the Falling Sun that the real Sun still shone high in the sky—an act of defiance. No one could have known for certain except her.

***

Upon her arrival back in the city, the people were almost done coalescing in silence and meditation. As she floated down and hovered just above the mass in her winged chariot, her mind was clear, focused on what was to come. The smooth finish of the chariot's brim occupied her antsy hands in anticipation for the moment. There, on the ground, was a single entity that was composed of common people, from both Lowhi and New Hope City, and the Fearnaughts. Such a gathering was most unique and rare: a drastic measure for a desired future.

At length, the crowd, now fully formed, awaited her command. Raising her hand to the sky, the people ascended themselves by ripping the ground beneath their feet as one slab upon which they all could stand. Zarra stepped onto the platform to act as the guide. To her right was her father, and to her father's right was her mother. To her left, Leader Loyaira stood boldly in an armor of well-prepared prognostication of how the event would play out. As the giant platform began to move forward, she whispered to her parents so no one else could hear. "Are you scared?"

They both looked into her emerald eyes. "Of course not . . . we're with our daughter," they replied.

As the giant mass drew closer to a perimeter in which their presence would then be known to the Falling Sun, every person wordlessly grabbed on to another to establish a network—like a web—between them all. As this was being done, everyone began a link with one another so that, in essence, a super link was created— that was the plan. Normally, linking was only done in drastic measures—to link with another is to sacrifice your internal worlds to those with whom you are linking. As such, it was rare and something not done carelessly. And, the more people who share the link, the more that is being surrendered. What they were doing was creating a singular entity with all of the people there through a link, which was dangerous. Because everyone was on the same wavelength, any one person then could disrupt the entire thing; it was a dire leap of faith across a canyon of uncertainty.

Zarra entered the link directly by connecting with her father and Leader Loyaira. Once there, a blank, white space in which there was nothing but the other people was the mental construct they all were now in.

"Think now of your most positive memory and share it!" Leader Loyaira shouted to all. "Think of that time in which you were most happy, whether that be an accomplishment, or a feeling, or a connection, or a moment in which everything made sense. Share it and let that positivity flood your senses and release it then to us!"

In accordance to the strategy, everyone then thought of their happiest moment and shared it so that the link they established between everyone was a fusion of positivity. Zarra thought of her dancing with her father to the tune of lively music, front and center on a stage, with friendly faces cheering her on. The music, the sweet music, flowed in her ears as the memory took hold. She was swirling and twirling around, letting her body and mind roam free with pleasure as her heart thumped with ecstasy. And in addition to her memory, many others filled with happiness, and meaning stormed within her and between one another. Within seconds, everyone had seen and experienced the happiest memories and thoughts of many souls, and the effect was astounding and immaculate.

The Falling Sun noticed their approach and swarmed to take up arms against them as they floated closer and closer to the heart of the scourge. Zark could be heard screaming, "Kill them! They are the aggressors now! Kill them! They have lost their protection from the Reaper now!" Each of the malign followers dressed in bloodred surrounded the floating fortress, sporadically zipping around it in the sky, attempting to strike at them. But, each attempt, either through raw Soula or physical manipulation of a deadly object, could not penetrate the Soula barrier projected by the connected. Throughout the battle, a hailstorm of various weapons rained down on the fortress by design of the Falling Sun, but the barrier would not break. "Separate them! Separate them!" Zark now commanded, seeing that their strength was bred from the connection they shared. With a new focus, the Falling Sun attempted to blast the people free from one another and destroy the platform upon which they all stood. But, through it all, the people of Lowhi and New Hope City and the Fearnaughts remained unscathed.

At long last, Zarra understood Deceus's words. Soullexes do not have to be something physical: they can be incorporeal, like memories and feelings! No wonder it was one of the first things he brought to her attention. Her Soullex, after all this time, was the music she heard, the dance she did, and the special moment she created between her father, herself, and strangers who became friends; he guessed that. With her now was a special Soullex that all of the people shared—positivity—and this grand guardian won over the negativity and maliciousness from the Falling Sun. In this moment of realization, she felt like she had now lived for the first time in all of her life. And that belief and feeling spread to everyone she had become one with. Using this surge, the thought of ending destruction and death and fear flooded the mass. Zarra then took that motivation and put her entire being—mind, soul, and heart—into the most powerful display of Soula she had ever done. From the roots, the trees below ripped out. The stones and rocks fell into the sky as the many plants too leapt forth from the only homes they had ever known. These organic materials shot out from below and encased each of the members of the Falling Sun individually, effectively trapping them. Only Zark and a few others, who now fled seeing their cause was lost, were able to effectively evade the constraints.

"Their belief is shattered, they are now scared, and their efforts are futile!" Leader Loyaira shouted. She turned to Zarra. "Their trifecta is null."

Zarra heard the words without truly listening to them; her mind was too focused to allow any remnants of the disastrous league to escape. To her right, she could have sworn that she heard her father, "It's all you! You can get them! Get them!" It was all her; this was what she had wanted. Days upon days of traversing the land, studying the evil, the deserted and deprived, came to her aid. And now she would be able to right her family's wrongs and save the future for those who could then live for it.

In her stride for actualization, the Tree of Live responded to her and granted her strength. From it, one of its branches departed and whistled through the air with ludicrous speed as its leaves rustled like fire. Fearnaught Zarra, feeling as though it was made to be an extension of her, guided it toward those who were escaping. As it got close to one, the many arms of the branch reached out and reeled them in, like tentacles. One by one, each of the Falling Sun was reeled in with the last capture being Zark, the first of the Falling Sun. Despite their adversary's best efforts, they could not muster the strength to escape their capture, for their willpower had evaporated into the air.

To Zarra's left, Leader Loyaira gave a small, mature nod as her parents hugged each other. Throughout the airwaves of the gray day, rejoicing rang true, filling the environs with splendor. At last, the crimson cloaks had been beaten, and Lowhi was saved. Not one casualty was had on either side of the battle. Zarra, noticing this, smiled with incredulity and happiness while the celebrations continued. When Deceus said that she would save everyone there, it was meant literally.

# Chapter 20 – Transcendence

The city of New Hope was imbued with a most colorful history. In times of pre-Imagerion, it was a center of conflict between people and ideals. It was here that Deceus Stormeus Maximus earned his revered reputation and iconic nicknames: the Angel and the Orator. What he did within the limits of the city was create stability, understanding, and positive change during a time of turbulence, ignorance, and pessimism. And in the center of this city stood a voluminous, worn-white marble building decorated with warrior statues; long threads of tossing red cloths; and reflective pools of crystal water surrounding its perimeter: the Coliseum. In Deceus's time, the House of Death, as it was sometimes referred to, was a symbol of conflict. Within its walls, criminals were forced to fight and slaughter one another for entertainment. As the city was divided into class districts at the time, the Coliseum, being at the center of the city, resembled the ever-waging war between the classes and interests of forces like politics. Especially within its walls, Deceus had influenced the city to ascend from its destitute ways onto a path of righteousness. In time, the Coliseum became a symbol of unity and conflict resolution.

Also symbolic of the city was its ever-present clouds; above, it was almost always overcast with a wild spectrum of gray. Every decade, the city would experience a storm like no other, a Great

Storm. Throughout several days, lightning would crack the sky, and thunder would shake the foundation of the world. It was in this gray sky that a throne seated a man clothed in white, hooded, and masked with a red stripe covering where his eyes would be. At first, he was in a rush to get there. However, on his way he thought it wise to slow down to better savor the precious moments. The Reaper, Rasck, now floated above the city with a self-prescribed air of an emancipator and saw it to be void of people. Throughout its perfectly blended streets of man-made design and nature, not a single soul could be found. But he was not looking for just anyone: he was looking for the one. And there was one place in which finding that one was certain: the Coliseum.

Now floating into the vast, open space of many seats and spectating areas, Rasck landed on the smooth, barren fighting floor. As he landed, he watched in apparent indifference as Deceus came out of one of the fighting floor's four gates—the north gate, to be exact. Hanging from his side was a sword that looked like a two-handed side sword with the length of a rapier.

"I'm glad you came, Iudex," Deceus stated as he walked across the floor and stopped directly across from the Reaper on the opposite side of the arena. In return, Rasck said nothing and did nothing but slouch slightly on this throne, Mercy laying across his lap. "When I first came to this city, it was slowly eroding from within . . . you knew that . . . but look at it now"—the Orator gestured—"the trees that have been planted where they never were are now full, the homes which had a chance to revive, the balance between us and the universe we were given. Wise men and women had worked without cease for a brighter future; it is for that reason those who live here now breathe fresh air, always. See the possible parallel?" Still, Rasck said nothing, as anticipated. "Even the Locket, which you now hold, was born here before this all changed. It has been thought—argued—that it was the first Soullex ever created. But, you knew that . . . and you probably know everything that I could say to try to convince you to stop . . . even . . . Verity."

"You will not speak of her," the heartless reply came, unforced but full of threat. "Nothing could explain her like how I knew . . ."

"You're right. I have no right to speak of her as if I knew her. But I know what she meant to you. That Locket was not intentionally made, Iudex: it was a by-product of love. The first Soullex of them all, one you have studied in your search of the past, was made for the purpose of understanding and bonding. That is why, should one look into its mirror and see their reflection, they will see their true self at that time—it is part of its Soula-derived power. And you know this too." He now slowed his speech to put special notice on the coming words. "But you dare not look into the mirror, because you know if

172

you did, you'd see as much of her as you would yourself. Your hearts"—the Angel reached to his chest—"beat to the same tune. Your souls, so connected and dependent on the other, fused into one. . . . You could look into the mirror. . . . You could fulfill your curiosity to see the man you became, to see if you're the hero you think you are . . . but you won't because you're scared . . . fearful you will only see half of yourself and once more reveal that pain that you have done so much to remove from this life."

"I already lost all that I feared to lose," a clean retort came. "You, on the other hand, have much to fear. . . . I can feel it." Deceus said nothing in response. "What was it that you once said? I think it was something along the lines of, 'The greatest gift that was given to the human race is the absence of meaning for our existence. Without determined meaning, we then have the ability to create meaning for ourselves.' Why, that's a terrible responsibility . . . a huge burden which leaves much, much room for negative emotions and streams of thought. You must know that I looked at your life considerably. Among only a select few, you were. Unfortunately, not even your actions came close to redeeming this world from the judgment the judge has rendered for it."

"Iudex . . . what would Verity say if she were here to see you now? Are you now who you must be? Is *this* the person she wanted you to be?" The Orator put special emphasis on his words.

The Reaper now stood, slowly, and glared from across the arena. "I've heard enough," he whispered. "You know what must happen. No doubt, that is why you brought the very sword you used in this stadium—a Soullex of yours, I'm sure. . . ." Deceus felt the presence of his blade more strongly. "As is this." A white-gloved hand now held out the Locket as if it was a pity offering. "You survived this once before, and now the House of Death seeks its reward after waiting all of these years. . . . See how things always come full circle." It was a simple comment but a devastating one, like telling a newborn that this was the beginning of their journey to eventual death.

The two faced off with the clouds swirling above, reflecting the gathering energy below. Deceus withdrew his sword, revealing an inscription on the blade, which read "FATEBREAKER," and called the Locket to him. As soon as the goldish-green object landed on his shoulders, his opponent began.

Rasck held out Mercy and concentrated a bullish blast on his target. His target, however, reacted in turn by doing the same and, in effect, canceled out the blast midway. "Well, well . . ." the Reaper chimed. He took the Scythe and slashed it through the air. The Coliseum reacted as if it itself was sliced diagonally and began to slide apart. Just as it all began tumbling upon itself, Deceus held it together using his power and repaired the damage as he began to rise to the top of the structure. While doing that and warding off new strikes from Mercy, he gathered water from the nearby ocean and aimed the mass toward the Reaper. Flying through the environs in the form of winding pillars made from the sea, the water swarmed Rasck with complex moves, like a series of punches from an experienced fighter. Each wave, however, was parried. Statues, now, were commanded to come to Rasck's aid and, one by one, the temporary minions approached Deceus. Flying back down to the fighting floor, Deceus addressed each nearby warrior with the tip of Fatebreaker. Ducking beneath a large swipe from an ax, he jabbed a breastplate and watched the figure fall apart into smaller pieces. Two now stepped forward, with spears, and lunged at him with intent to kill. Slicing off both hazardous tips, Deceus thrust out his free hand and made a clutching motion with his fist, effectively demolishing the two attackers into a pile of rubble. As more and more statues filtered into the arena, Deceus held Fatebreaker to the sky and swirled it around. With the motion, the clouds began to swirl into the stadium in the form of a tornado. While both the Reaper and the Angel shielded themselves from the fierce winds, the statues commanded by Mercy were swept off into nothingness. Seeing the need for a new approach, Rasck cut through the tornado and brought the winds to a cease and the clouds receding into the sky. Blowing off the gates of the fighting floor, he then bid every historic weapon in the building to come forth. Pouring out, they formed around him in an intimidating display of controlled precision. They came at Deceus in intervals, stabbing, slashing, and bludgeoning the defensive shield of Soula that he conjured in response. The raining metal sung as the sharpened edges stung and rebounded off Deceus's protection. After granting himself asylum for a few moments, he gathered strength and released the energy, blowing all of the Reaper's threats away. He then looked across the arena and saw his opponent sitting down once more. Throughout the struggle, neither of the two had been touched by the other.

"Let us be honest. We both are, after all, honest, angry men," Rasck said with coolness. "Isn't that right? The thing is, my anger will lead to the end of all of our problems. . . . Yours will allow them to continue, to persist, transform . . . You think this will end here? Hmph. Hardly. Haven't you heard? The world's falling apart. People, now, are turning on one another, concerned about the current state of affairs and where we all are heading. I won the *instant*—the *instant*—I was made into this." He waved his hand over himself in a boastful way. "The world, you see, is like a glass ball. Drop one stone on it anywhere"—he patted his throne—"and watch it all shatter. I don't have to follow through and see my mission through—though I will—because the people will do it for me. If anything, my passion will become easier, in time. Perhaps I should just wait, for now.

176

We're all selfish creatures, really. So enticed by self-continuance, and competition, and whatever captures our imaginations throughout the day. Even sacrifices by *noble* men and women have been lost through the translations of human behavior and ignorance. You have not seen our past like I have." He raised himself and Mercy once more. Then he increased his volume with each sentence. "I win because I have the belief that what I do is *right*. In fact, I know it is right, *inevitable*. I have the emotion to match that vision. We will know serenity! We will no longer know struggle, only *peace*! I have put forth the effort my entire life to make things better for *everyone*! You must see! *You haven't felt the pain I have!*" The sky tinted red, and all of that focused anger pent up inside Iudex released in the form of an epic blast of Soula directed at the Angel.

For several seconds, the deafening roar of the blast wiped out any other sound that could have possibly tried to outdo the explosion. It shot up to the heavens, far out to the forests and mountains, and dove into the deep oceans. A storm of dirty air was conjured up in the Coliseum, and Rasck's visibility was severely reduced. Without his eyes, however, he could still sense a living, human presence. In fact, he now felt . . . two.

"You're right, Reaper. . . . He has felt a much different pain." To the side, the silhouetted figure of another appeared. The ghostly figure stepped through and revealed itself to be Zarra.

"You," Rasck simply stated, recognizing her as the one who delivered him here. "Do not dare portray me to be the villain in this. . . . Only those who allow this world to exist are worthy of the title."

"You're not a villain, just someone who lost everything you loved, as did Deceus," Zarra said, uninhibited by the flying dust and dirt. "When I first met him, one of the first things he told me was that he froze himself so that he could come back to the world should we ever need him. At the time, I thought that to be only that, nothing more. But as time drew on, and he taught me, I soon realized what that truly meant through insights of my own. Freezing himself prohibited him from being with his family throughout their lives as they aged. It prevented him from finding love and doing the things he enjoyed. Deceus sacrificed all of his happiness so that the world's happiness could have a chance to persist if it was ever in mortal peril." The Reaper remained motionless during the monologue, grasping Mercy with vying fingers. "From your birth to childhood to where you were just before you became the Reaper, you had everything you could have possibly wanted. The world blessed you. Deceus, however, never had anyone who believed in him when he was young. And the world constantly turned on him, making his situations more difficult. Yet, you are now the one who seeks to end all life, and he is the one who aims to save it."

Rasck held out Mercy. "Never. Never . . . no! What you say is to perpetuate the inevitable, to allow history to repeat itself to pain, suffering! This cycle, our history, must stop, for all of our sakes!" Using some of the rubble from the fallen statues, Rasck directed the debris to form cuffs around Zarra's wrists and ankles so that she could not move. "Tell me, Fearnaught, why do you live?" he commanded as Mercy shimmered.

Zarra didn't respond for several seconds as the dust and dirt started to settle. Steadily, visibility became clearer. But this was peripheral to the conversation between the two souls in the House of Death. "The truth is," Zarra stated, "I haven't." The Reaper shuddered and refocused on her. "The truth is," she continued, "that many of us never do. It's not uncommon for us to live our entire lives without actually ever living. I . . . I know I haven't. Not until just now, at least. If you stop to think about it . . . how many of us stop our lives, no matter where we are, and understand our situation? To understand what it is that we are made of and how the heavens themselves and the stars in space constitute our very beings? How often is it that the world doesn't seem scary to us or that something is going wrong, somewhere, somehow, with someone or something? Think about the conflicts we have between each other . . . within ourselves . . . for what we choose to live for. How often is it that we choose to believe something without truly understanding why? How often do we feel without knowing why we feel what we do? For what do we put our efforts to and should we even? The truth is . . . not many of us ever live, and I haven't even started until now. But I'll tell you why I'm starting to: I'm starting so that I can help everyone to live. It's what you did and it's what you continue to live for . . . and without Iudex's mentality to enable life, *your* mentality to enable life, Verity wouldn't have ever lived. And for that, you must be happy."

As normal visibility returned entirely, Deceus appeared in the sky above them both, unscathed from Rasck's blast. On a cloud made from the local environs he stood; behind him, the clouds aligned in such a manner that made it appear that he had wings. "Our goal is to help people who have never lived to live," the Angel said.

"That'll never happen," Rasck retorted, flabbergasted at what he saw and wondering whether his eyes were deceiving him.

"Perhaps it can . . . perhaps it can't. There's only one way to find out."

"What are you proposing?"

"A solution. You think the world must stop because of our inevitable future and the cyclical nature of our existence, which ends in heartbreak. . . . What I am offering you is finality. Give me the chance to end the cycle and enable this world's people to live. Should I succeed, the cycle will stop, and the inevitability of pain, suffering, and futility will be eradicated. Should I fail, you will have all that you need to end the people of this planet personally. Either way, your mission will be complete."

The Reaper paced for a moment, contemplating. "And what will I do during this time?"

"Whatever you want to so long as you don't interfere to give me a true, unbiased chance."

Again, silence came as Rasck meditated on the offer. He couldn't kill Deceus, and Deceus wouldn't kill him, even if he could. They would fight until they both collapsed from either exhaustion or starvation, neither of them truly advancing on the other, in a stalemate of the ages. Although what he was proposing would allow for more negativity, it at least would be an inexorable outcome in his favor. The Reaper turned to the Angel. "I accept," he said. "But, when the time comes for me to eradicate life in all capacities—which it will—my strike will be immediate, swift, and uninhibited."

"Of course," Deceus agreed.

The Reaper then returned to his throne, looked at both Deceus and Zarra once more, and then floated into the gray sky.

# Chapter 21 – Contingency

With the Reaper now out of sight, Deceus took a deep breath and floated up into the stands of the Coliseum and sat down. At his side, he placed Fatebreaker, his sword. Zarra came and joined him. Together, the two looked down into the fighting floor and saw scars of the previous conflict, which now had afflicted the previously unblemished display: a symbolic reference to the structure's jaded past.

"That was a terrific answer you gave him," Deceus stated.

"The answer to why I live?" she asked in return.

"Yes," he affirmed, feeling proud of her. A second later, he asked, "On your way in, did you notice the city?"

"It looks very pleasant . . . well, minus this part now."

He gave a small exhale of acknowledgment. "It wasn't always like this . . . none of it."

She looked at him. "I know it wasn't always like this. But it now is because a long time ago *someone* decided to make a change. And that change, now, is reflected many, many years later. I can see why you wanted him here."

"All of our actions have a bearing on the future, and we should act accordingly."

"You also wanted me to be here."

"I did."

"And yet you only told me to do what I thought was right."

"Yes."

She thought for a second about what that meant. The silence between the two was natural, as were the clouds overhead that continued to vibe. "We saved everyone at Lowhi. . . . And I say 'we' because I was not alone."

"Of course you did."

All around, the season of spring blossomed in the form of swaying trees, calming breezes, and color-splashed plants. "Can you see the future?" she asked with seriousness, thinking about everything he had said over their journey together. "You seem to be gifted with foresight."

He picked up Fatebreaker and began inspecting it; its material gleamed, even though there wasn't any direct light on it to make it so. "No. I cannot see the future, but I can shape it . . . as can you. As can anyone who decides to."

"Then how did you know that I'd come back, especially at the right time?"

"Trust."

"That's it . . . a leap of faith?"

"If we cannot trust people to do the right thing, Zarra, the world will not last. Rasck is betting against people, whereas I am willing to bet for them. Humans are not perfect. . . . They never will be. So, we can either choose to think of others as unworthy and incapable, to live in fear and eternal anxiety, or we can choose to trust them to, in time, live up to the standard of hope. I will not lie to you: our faith will be tested, sometimes each and every day. But we must have faith. Without that possibility, what we are now will never be able to become what we may be." He held up Fatebreaker, allowing its full length and lethalness to display itself. "This is a weapon. Throughout time, it has been seen as a weapon, an agent of destruction. And yet, it has saved lives without taking one. Think about what that means."

"And why did you let him go?"

"Because I believe that the world needs him."

"Needs him?" she asked, allowing the shock to be reflected in her voice. "The world is falling apart because of him. People are turning on one another across the globe, and conflicts are on the rise that could devastate our very foundations of humanity . . . and you say we all may need him?"

"We are all protagonists, each and every one of us. Iudex's story with us has not yet run its course."

"And what will become of him? You just challenged him in a contest to see whether or not life should exist."

"Yes, and in doing so I not only stopped him but saved many others from having to face him while allowing myself the time to address our worldwide problems."

"So that was the end goal?" she spoke. "After all this time, that was the hope?"

He nodded.

A moment of silence followed. "So," she gathered, "the world is falling apart and people are turning on one another. Soon, all will likely be chaos. Rasck is roaming free. Your goal is to prove to him that life is worth existing and that the cyclical nature of our very existence can be broken. In doing so, he will no longer have the means to destroy everything . . . or, should the mission end in failure, he will be able to destroy everything much easier."

"The cycle he believes is real isn't real. In actuality, the world is not becoming a worse place, it's becoming a *better* place."

"How can you say that after all that we have seen and after all that has happened and will happen?"

The Angel paused, staring fixedly into the Coliseum's fighting floor. "As in the past, as of now, as in the future, we will be bombarded with negativity. We will talk about the problems we all face, imagine the fires we will have to subdue and the seemingly insurmountable odds. It all becomes a ubiquitous force and is often all that we can then see. I learned to see past all of that. I learned to ignore the noise, all of the speculation and static. Instead of seeing all of that, I began to look at people. In time, I soon saw that we—as a whole—are advancing. While there will be those outliers who showcase themselves, the cycle the Reaper speaks of is being broken each day. To the untrained eye, it is hard to see. To the closed mind, it is hard to conceive. But believe me, the world is and has been on a positive trend upward, not in a negative cycle. . . . We just all must ensure it stays that way." Here, he paused. Then he began to recite something Zarra had never heard before.

"Begin, now, the Darkest Light

Where good and bad meet right

We, humans, in our conquest strife

What will we do with our life

Though through the night we fight

Until we can, at last, end in right

From birth till death, we seek our way

Pray, we may, that we last the day

Check your heart, check your mind

In yourself, you will find

Deep, The Darkest Light

With that, pride insight

Imagine world

Imagine you

See the polarity

Hear the hot melody

Decide, then, who you be

And ascend, eternity"

"What was that?" the Fearnaught asked.

"A critically edifying poem."

"What does it—" Zarra began to ask but stopped, realizing that she had to determine what it meant for herself.

Deceus took note of her realization. "You should know, we think of the trifecta as the main power of Soula. But an inconsiderate amount of attention is given to something just as powerful: imagination. Imagination is the bridge between what is and what could be—it is everything. We need it more than any of us know—I especially."

"Think of what you want, and then make it happen. . . . So, what do you see when you imagine?"

"A world much different from the one the Reaper thinks he wants."

"Seems like the odds are stacked against success."

"Consider the world to be against you because it wouldn't be fair any other way."

Fearnaught Zarra laughed. Despite the overwhelming odds, she was suddenly feeling at peace. "And what makes you think that thought can become true?"

"I cannot say definitively. I have my logic, and I have my intuition. . . . But, I believe, it will depend primarily on one thing."

Zarra didn't ask what that one thing was. Why didn't she have to ask? Because she knew—we all know. Choose not to exist—live. Choose not to fear—hope. Choose not to succumb—withstand. Choose not to hate—love. Choose not to take—give. Choose life. And then, ask yourself why. And then, transcend.

# NOTES

# NOTES

www.ingramcontent.com/pod-product-compliance
Lightning Source LLC
Chambersburg PA
CBHW060106260626
47160CB00005B/1819